Instinct

short stories

Instinct

— short stories —

Vivi Merrill

Instinct: Short stories
© Vivi Merrill
ISBN: 9798781447640
First edition, 2021

Cover design and illustrations
Isabella Manjarrés Melo @imailustracion
Layout
Hugo H. Ordóñez Nievas

Suggestions and comments
vivimerrill.usa@gmail.com

Social networks

vivimerrill

Editorial advice

Printed in Mexico
December, 2021

Recognizing and accepting
my own madness, brings me
closer to the sanity of others...
that we are all.

About the Stories

Can fictional stories based upon significant events in the real life of a neighbor, a friend, or a family member be put into the hands of my readers? That is precisely the question these twelve short stories pose. The book is an invitation to reflect through the extraordinary anomalies of everyday life.

We can relate to scenarios such as a woman swallowed up by loneliness, an adolescent who gasped her last breath in the hands of a stranger, a mother trapped in heartbreaking mourning over the death of her little one, or the mind of a man condemned forever into the events of his childhood. These and other short narratives that dwell in our universe, are included. They are windows into the human condition that invite readers to enter the inner complex world of other human beings.

Instinct is a book that intends to awake in the reader the psychological world of the self, which we all are a part of. It is an invitation to understand the everyday struggles of others in an unexpected, unconventional way.

Recognizing that constant search for the human wellness and its shapes is a challenge. As the writer Octavio Paz says: "In order for me to be, I have to be another, to come out of myself, to look for myself among the others, the others who are not if I do not exist, the others who give me full existence."

Through these short stories, the reader will explore the unique world of each of the characters. Risk, madness, and the alienated mind are some scenarios from the anguish of personal liberation or distorted reality.

In my psychological practice, I have found human beings who have lived with unbearable loss, mental illness, or an unsolvable conflict. These experiences, hidden behind the mask of everyday life, become visible through literature and come to disrupt the collective mind.

To all of you who suffer my
passion for literature.

Stories

"The inner voice of the different"

The Feat

Only that which never stops hurting,
remains in the memory

Michel Foucault

He thought he was in the trunk of a vehicle because his body was violently spinning and thumping against the hard surfaces which surrounded him. A blow to his back, his head, his ribs, then suddenly—wham! The chaos stopped, and he returned to a central position. The duct tape that bound his mouth shut made him feel desperate. He lost hope that someone would come to his aid.

He squirmed forcefully. He could not move his arms, and while trying to do so, he wriggled around like larvae. He thought about how his day started; he wasn't sure. He tried to remember if he had left the eggs on the stove...

Another sharp turn of the vehicle, another blow to the head; pain again.

Something smelled foul. He stopped to concentrate on the origin of that rotten smell, which reminded him of the latrine of his childhood ... Fifteen people, including his brothers, parents, cousins, uncles and grandparents, lived in a two-room hut on the outskirts of town and excreted in the same pit.

He began to hear indistinguishable voices. It was hard for him to identify whose they were; there were two or three. Squeaks of wheels and shouts of authority crept in. He struggled to move his arms again, but without success. He decided to escape his confinement using his legs. He curled them up as if in a fetal position and slammed the soles of his feet against what he thought was the center of the trunk. A thunderous metallic noise followed. He took the opportunity to crawl into the void he had created, realizing that it was his chance to flee. However, in his attempt to escape, he collided with something indistinguishable. He fell backwards, but managed to stand up quickly. A stabbing pain in his right ankle made him limp; however, with short and unsteady steps, he persevered with his escape.

Everything was dark, but he managed to perceive some slow movements in the shadows. He had finally accomplished the feat of freeing himself. He took a few steps to orient himself and felt what seemed to be an old wall. Reaching his arms up, he held onto it. The wall crumbled a little, and he looked at the floor to see that some bugs had fallen along with the rubble. He thought again of that morning… The stove and the eggs… He was again worried about having left the gas stove on.

Then the vertigo hit, and he grew more and more confused.

He looked at his wrist to check the time with his watch, but could not find it. He noticed that a pinkish rash was forming on his arm, right where it had touched the wall. His skin itched, and he felt an excruciating charge of heat. The rash then turned a sickly, brownish color. It seemed as if a welt was growing under his skin, demanding to leave his arm. He was paralyzed with fear; he thought that he was suffering from some sort of deadly infection. He remembered Gregor Samsa[1]: if only he had gotten out of bed at four o'clock every morning; if only he had forced himself to turn his back to be on the right side of the bed!

Suddenly, he entered a deep state of apprehension and loneliness. He felt like Samsa. Lost in the shadows of a room, he calculated the distance that separated him from the wall and the metal door. The room was extremely remote, inhospitable, empty. Hopelessness began to consume him.

A dull gray cloud rose behind his head. He turned suspiciously to get a good look. He was sure that it was another ruse orchestrated by the kidnapper: now, the captor wanted to control his thinking and get information from him regarding the World Health Organization. The pain in his ankle distracted him from this thought, and seconds later, he heard someone try to open the door. He froze and watched it closely. Decades of waiting passed. He was surprised that he could see the door so clearly.

The air began to smell of burnt eggs and dirt. He quickly ran to the metal door, but could not stop it. It was a gas leak, and soon someone was going to enter the room with a match causing everything to explode! Quickly, he tried to find the safety knob, but the door was smooth. It only had a small hole patterned with bars at the top. He couldn't reach it!

He sat on his knees trying to hold the door with his back. It was hard to breathe. His eyes began to wander, and heart palpitations choked his chest. His dry throat knotted. Tired of fighting, he tried to scream, but his voice never came out.

When I entered to the dorm, Samuel was passed out against the door of the stark room. He had hit the walls until he bled. The straitjacket was stained red with blood, and the physical ravages of his mental transformation were clearly visible. It was evident that the visit of his relatives had produced a host of negative symptoms. I had warned them, but, as is well known, denial in family members is the mother of all crises!

Rocco

Man is a wicked being by nature, and
although we are rational beings, this
same perversion inhibits any trace of
reason in us.

"The Proletarian Child"
Osvaldo Lamborghini

When I was about ten years old, I graduated the fifth grade with nothing less than a B. For such a great accomplishment, I received a puppy. I was the only one with good enough grades to satisfy my parents, who by then, were content with any of their children passing.

That very same summer, after my last day of school, the dog came home. In the living room, my brothers argued about how unfair my reward was. To them, I was the rudest, most misbehaved sibling of us all. I cannot confirm nor deny that. However, I was the only one that passed my classes.

"Leave little Fernando alone, he earned the right to his dog, and he will do what he wants with it. You kids have to learn to work like he does," my mother said. No one argued.

My mom and I named the dog Rocco. At first, he followed me around every corner. Then, he spent most of his time napping and eating. He ate constantly, more than a starving man stranded on a deserted island. Since he was mine, I taught him that I was his master and that he must obey me. Otherwise, he will be punished. This is how I trained him.

Several days of more training and doggy games passed. I enjoyed walking him in the park; we played catch and kept each other company. I preferred being with him rather than with my brothers or my classmates. In the afternoons, we would go hunting and chase stray cats. Once, we caught a Siamese cat. Its hair was shiny, and it had a cute bell attached to its collar. Rocco chased it down and pinned it against the wall, but he didn't dare bite. I kicked the cat so that Rocco would learn to be strong and respected. The cat whimpered, and Rocco hid behind me, with his tail between his legs. I did not like that from my own dog; enraged, I punished him. I left him tied up, without any food or water for a short while.

Soon, I began to notice that Rocco was hanging around a little too close. He was so close, I was almost walking on top of him. He made me trip over everything. "Get off, weak mutt! Good for nothing!" I yelled at him. In fact, I began to yell at him at least twenty times a day. This dog was afraid of rain, wind, and even noise. It started to bother me a lot. Begging for more food was his favorite thing to do. I had to clean his poop, bathe him, and force him to sleep in his doggy house outside. The foolish mutt was even scared of the dark! Ugh, I could no longer bear how he constantly got in my way. Being around him always put me in a bad mood.

That's when I came up with a plan for the nuisance. My brothers didn't want to help. "That little thing is yours, isn't it?" they told me smugly.

Rocco stopped getting between my legs when I cut his nails short. Maybe a bit too short. His paws were caked in blood. I bathed them with alcohol, so they wouldn't get infected. In fact, I dunked each entire leg in alcohol!

Maga, my younger sister, watched silently from across the kitchen. Tears ran down her cheeks as she shook her head from side to side. She was soft spoken. I called her "the freak-show". She was so easy to ignore. I was proud of how I made that burdensome beast stop bumping into me all over the house. I finally got him to lay down.

After I cut his nails, the damn dog would whine all day. I couldn't bear it. Mom would kill me if I cut out his tongue, but I did find a sneaky way to shut him up. The dog no longer barked or whined after that. I did not tell anyone, only I knew what caused his silence. A mischievous giggle slipped from my lips.

The wounds were getting worse every day. The cowardly dog could no longer stand up to urinate or poop, so I had to take him out to the yard. I tied him close to the ground; he did everything there, even crawl in his own shit. Within a week, he stopped eating and drinking, and was beginning to rot. You cowardly dog! Getting these grades was a curse. I will never be a good student again.

—"It's about time, Fernando, someone else is waiting for their turn. You know what it's like here," the psychiatrist interrupted. The guard tapped on the iron fence to announce that it was time to return to my cell.

"Thank you doctor, I liked this game. This is just one of many stories from my childhood. Maybe I'll write a book. You know doctor, it's already on my bucket list."

Raindrops

Our group was very close. The card game took place every afternoon at one of our houses; we took turns hosting it during the week.

Mrs. Gordillo was the kind of woman who adorned herself with jewels and heels to go out and play cards with her friends in the garden of the houses. She was among the most particular of all. She always wore a black hat with a narrow brim, one of those from the fifties (according to her), because at any moment it could rain, and the raindrops would ruin her makeup.

Her husband, a wealthy man with little free time, was usually absent from home working long hours. They never had children. She had a problem in the womb, due to a syndrome named Asherman or something like that.

Mrs. Gordillo was of extravagant tastes and divinely splendid. That day, she went to the supermarket so that in the afternoon when we sat down to play at her house, we would have wine, marzipan, sandwiches, and cake.

That afternoon, it rained. A tremendous storm fell, and the lady could not prevent her makeup from being ruined with so much water. From my window, I saw her arrive; she came in slowly, with a pale and contracted face. I ran to her house to find out what had happened, and of course, offer my help for the card game that afternoon.

In horror, I saw that the drops of water had gotten into the pores of her head! Truly! She was crying uncontrollably as she shook her head vigorously, hopping on one leg, first the right, then the left.

Already the three of us, her friends, were accompanying her. Her husband had not arrived, and night had fallen. Her composure had transformed: her pale face, dilated pupils, and slow pulse described the symptoms of a high-risk state of panic.

The news of a dead man had come in the newspaper. Due to the torment of a drop of water on his head, despair had made him crazy. He had lost his wits, and with it, his life. That was what worsened Mrs. Gordillo's belief that raindrops could flood her brain. She always argued that it was her makeup, but what she really feared was that her brain would drown.

We were worried about her, but all of us accompanied her as good friends. The first thing we did was connect a drain that reached her ear and emptied into a bucket on the floor, which did not work because barely half a drop of rain came out.

I had the idea to put a foam helmet on her and leave her head hanging from the side of the bed for a while. That method did work, as the foam got wet and we all saw an improvement in Mrs. Gordillo's expression.

She did not speak. Her eyes were not working, her skin was taking the tone of puddled water, and her husband still had not arrived. The situation was desperate. As dawn fell, I saw how her eyes moved. From the bottom of her throat came a slight, very high-pitched snore. I approached with fear, and seeing her in such a dire state, I made the decision that we could not wait any longer for her husband; something had to be done!

Between the three of us, we tied her to the bed, so that the discomfort of the procedure would not cause her to move. We readied the materials and the medicine, and we entrusted ourselves to the archangel of miracles and the mother of the universe.

When the hose entered the ear canal, we had to hold her down even tighter. We pushed the probe forcefully, in order to break the tympanic membrane. We passed it from end to end, through the frontonasal canal, and there we stopped it so that it absorbed the water that had entered through the pores of her head. It was working very well in our eyes. Her pallor took on a different color, something like a pale green, but it looked better. Suddenly, her eyes began to move in all directions and her body stood up as if giving us signals that almost all the water was coming out. She was cooperating. We held her head, body, and limbs as the bucket filled with water. It no longer seemed like rain, since the water had passed through her body, giving it a soft, reddish color. Mrs. Gordillo was no longer so rigid. On the contrary, her body gradually gave way.

When the movement stopped, we felt more relieved. She smelled somewhat of acid, like formaldehyde, but being able to help her comforted us. At the first calls of the rooster, we each went back home so that she could rest. She looked immobile and at peace. I was the last to leave her. Her husband was the first to find her in her new condition.

The
Beast

I found you in the whiteness of the morning, there in that little store, sitting with that wanting look. I invited you to walk in the park, and you accepted. I will always thank you.

We walked for a while. With your worried little face, you told me that you hadn't been to school because, that day, you were in the mood for something else. Then, I, an opportunist, desired to capture your mind and become your friend.

We arrived at the park near the cathedral where the willows keep secrets and loving couples meet to engage in mischief. But we weren't dating, and you didn't know how to engage in mischief. I threw you into the grass. I remember your look of surprise. To my advantage, the wind forcefully swept your long hair into your mouth and into your eyes. You no longer spoke; you no longer saw.

A trickle of blood came out of your vulva, and your skin turned cadaverous. Your tight eyes wept silently, but I no longer knew if it was from pain or from youthful passion. You wanted to move, but the weight of my body prevented it. Already, my skin was under your nails, and my breath within your lungs.

You were muttering something through your teeth —I'm not sure if about school or your bike— I silenced your moans with my hands. Your gaze paled, and your legs were immobile.

My hands will always be imprinted on your languid, white neck. Abandoned, your soul remained between two willows. Satisfied, I returned my eyes to see you one last time; now without a pulse, your darkened lips did not attract my attention.

In the distance, I saw smoke. Black smoke. I hid you behind the branches of the willows. Nobody saw us. You remained inert in nothingness.

"From Myself"

The Wait

No one should be alone
in their old age. But it is inevitable
that this is the case.

Ernest Hemingway

When my eyes opened, I looked at the clock and indeed, it was four thirty in the morning. At my age this routine was becoming more and more predictable. I reached for the water on the nightstand, clumsily knocking the glass to the floor. With trepidation, I tried to stand up faster, but couldn't. I had learned to be careful and not expose myself to accidents; my bones would no longer endure one more fall. The day promised to be special because I would see the only man who listened to me. In fact, he empathically accepted my ailments, my emotional insufficiency, or my complaints. For a whole month, I kept hoping to talk to him, the day was in front of me. Slowly and carefully, I scooped up the broken glass and went into the kitchen to make my tea.

I gathered up my hair; in the morning the odor it expels makes me nauseous, is a smell of grease and sweat, mixed with the patchouli that I spray on my pillow to sleep at least a few hours at a time. I showered, put talcum powder on my body, and finished my tea.

By six in the morning I was ready, in my white thread lace dress, which had always evoked such cutting remarks from my son. Especially when in his drunken double vision, he missed took it for a mundane bathrobe or the like, and berated for my disreputable choice. But even still, it was my favorite dress.

I sat on the rustic wooden bench next to my fireplace, and slowly reclined on the backrest in a stiff frozen position, I did not voluntarily lift a finger again. I waited, waited, and waited, without even drinking a drop of water, until just before two in the afternoon, when I would see my counselor.

The appointment itself was always the same routinely. I was looking forward to this day, because, for me, it was a relief, a huge breath of oxygen. I was compelled to tell him that I had fallen, and I had no choice but to wait for my son. When he arrived, he was so inebriated at the time, that he tripped over the crystal lamp, which for so many years I had scrupulously cared for, since it was a gift from my beloved deceased. My son threw up on the floor, at the side of me, and I thought he would swallow the vomit because he was also hyperventilating. My cries for help were so loud that finally, my neighbor had no choice but to come to my aid.

Once in the therapist office, the secretary made me sit on a modern padded sofa, the kind that you see in upscale, decorative magazines. She offered me a Vogue which I did not accept, at this point it was no longer anticipation; it was anxiety and the mounting fear of forgetting something. I had waited twenty minutes before seeing him, and he greeted me attentively, with a firm, but empathetic, affable voice.

"Hi Anna, how have you been feeling this last month? How are things with your son?"

I looked at him, and with a doubtful and trembling voice, I began to speak. I spoke of myself, of my loneliness, of the nocturnal emptiness since the death of my husband. I spoke of the long nights during which I planned my meeting with him, and I also spoke of how I dreamed this meeting with un-fold. I told him how my wrinkled skin felt dry from the wind in the fall; I told him many random things. Every now and then he would stop to see my face, my expression, as if I was some-how waiting for his approval to continue speaking.

He said: "Continue, woman; continue."

And then he wrote on his computer. Sometimes he would open a small pocket book and draw.

"Continue Anna, continue," he said.

I had time to remember a sister-in-law who died long ago. Between bouts of crying and sobbing, I spoke of the pain of losing my son in life or, better yet, of his life lost to alcohol. I lamented the anguish that it gave me not being able to walk my dog "Miki". I talked, talked and talked non-stop, but I for-got everything I had thought to say to him.

Oh, and it was not necessary to tell him about how my bladder problem was progressing or tell him that patchouli is no longer good for anything. Because just when I was about to tell him, he looked at the clock that was strategically placed on the side table with him next to the sofa. He turned his gaze to me and quickly noticed my soaked dress, and on the couch, a large dark circle revealing my problem. Was this the end of that white thread lace dress being my favorite?

He closed his computer and said, "It is time, Anna; we must stop here."

I left in silence, walking alone with my thoughts and feeling so ashamed.

Through my eyes

They really are creatures of a violent
world, biologically speaking.

Steven Pinker

The only punishment I had in my existence was on a day that began as an ordinary day. Calm and peace reigned, which are the most extraordinary gifts of nature. We had come just a short time ago to live in Tamaron, a city where the citizens love their pets.

I remember well that day; it was about nine o'clock. I had already gone out for a walk with my mom and had breakfast too. The morning was cool, the trees danced with the sunlight. I wanted to lie down by the pool for a while; I liked to take a morning nap. The sun's rays caressed my short fur. I felt the air hug me warmly, and there I lay, peacefully still, dozing on the bed of grass.

Suddenly, I heard a noise from the fence next to the garage. My instincts prompted me to find out what was going on. With curiosity, I walked a little towards the street in the direction of the neighbor's fence. We had just moved into this house and didn't know a lot about neighborhood safety. I took advantage of the fact that half of the wooden fence was lying on the grass; and I jumped on it. The neighbor's garage door was open, it was easy for me to go in to say hello, I always liked people: I was known to have a docile, cheerful, and sociable character. This particular old man was surprised when he saw me, and I sensed fear from his reaction that I did not like.

I did not feel confidence in his look. He approached me; I do not know why. I took three steps back; the man did not stop. He kept walking towards me with his arm extended like someone who wants to touch my head: suddenly I felt imminent fear. Out of the corner of my eye, just a little bit, I turned my head to measure the distance back to the door; it wasn't much. When I saw the neighbor's hand on top of my eyes, my heart leapt in anguish, and I no longer held back! From my throat a thick, deep growl came out.

My mouth opened intimidatingly; the corners became visible and drew two large curves in the expression of my face and teeth, broadly showing their most effective threatening position: teeth, fangs and molars appeared in defensive function. I quickly pounced on the neighbor's body. He, visibly scared, backed off and started yelling things that were incomprehensible, verbal discords. My stress was running rampant because I don't like to feel so vulnerable.

When my dad came running, I finally let go of the old man's pants, which, embedded in my fangs and forced me to turn my head from side to side without achieving my total freedom. On the one hand, the frantic dancing of the neighbor's body, on the other, the slapping of my dad in my body, and I, with all my strength backed towards the exit. My heart throbbed at a thousand revolutions per second while the three of us tried to get out of this trouble in which circumstances had put us.

The neighbor called 911 and the firefighters, the ambulance, and three cars of policemen arrived. Everyone, plus a few gossipers from the block, had to wait for the man from the Animal Humane Society to arrive. He had brought an arrest warrant for dangerous pets like me, that threatened the safety of the neighborhood. When they arrived, the order ruled that I should be transferred immediately to the "End of life

Services". In other words, they were going to take my life because I was a dangerous breed of dog with high risk to the community. My human family had no opportunity to defend my actions.

We, canines, have no voice to explain, to argue or to defend an incident, and my family wasn't present at the time, so they were not allowed to intercede or protect the life of their pet.

From the window of the patrol car that was transporting me, I saw how my little brother, my mom and some neighbors were crying inconsolably. Of course, the neighbors gathered a considerable sum of money for a private cremation, it was the payment of my euthanasia. According to those neighbors who valued my welfare, the pain would be lessened if it happened as quickly as possible, and they reminded my owners in their condolence note that, in Tamarón, citizens did, indeed, love their pets.

The Sleeping Monster

The great monster had always slept on the outskirts of town. It addressed the horizon with arrogance, a lone white horn accentuating its magnificence. About forty-eight kilometers away, silent and arrogant, it hoped we'd just keep to ourselves. Drowsy from the recent vast storm and lulled to complacency by the sway of the rice and cotton plantations, we did not notice the tremendous danger ahead of us.

It had been asleep for sixty-nine years, struggling to pacify its dreams of freedom. Dreams to complete its nature, to rain down fury and pain. No one could interpret its urgency, its voice, nor its imminence.

It was Wednesday. The quiet of the night was threatening. After nine o'clock, the corner store still sold chocolate and achira biscuits. On the way home, I stopped by to grab breakfast for the next morning. Early tomorrow we'll leave for school, just like every other day. "Go, get ready for bed Omaira; it's getting late, daughter," I said uneasily, without knowing why. My grandmother called it having a "hunch".

My girl searched for Winnie the Pooh pajamas insistently, opening the wardrobe drawers, the nightstand, and even rummaging under her bed. Sadly, she did not find them. She looked at me with tender eyes pleading for help. I handed her the beloved pajamas and her sweet stuffed dog that she slept with.

Two hours later, I found myself restless in my sleep; I lay under a waning moon, silent and languid. It was almost too quiet.

In my dream stage, I saw myself running up the gloomy, jagged mountain. Elusive shadows chased me; I couldn't even tell whether they were trees, animals, or people. My heart was pounding anxiously, beads of sweat dripped down my face. I heard screams crying out for help behind me. A chill of terror invaded my defenseless body. I was afraid and uncertain of everything. I heard the desperate screams of people or the anguished bellowing of cattle; it was the sound of agony. I felt between life and death.

The monster vomited its black fury. Blowing unrelenting behind my back, it almost caught up with me. We ran even faster.

Like rivers of thick water, we all ran at breakneck speed. The night was dark and cold; the monster pursued. With ease, it brushed away entire trucks and roofs alike. It dragged its relentless rocks and fire over what used to be our precious town.

I didn't stop to think. I didn't try to help the animals. I didn't even think about going home to help my daughter... I couldn't anymore. I was already consumed by the mud, like lahars in the twilight. There were no longer clouds. There was no longer a horizon. There was no longer even the sustenance of air. I closed my eyes and coiled my body like an earthworm trapped in its predator's grip. I felt myself burn and float into the air, into the mud... everywhere. I wasn't sure when I realized I wasn't dreaming.

Between mud and ash, I was struck by one instinct: the need to struggle for my own life. Almost instantly, my mind silenced all other thoughts, emotions, and attachments. I was in a naked existence, without a daughter, without a husband, and without a home, I looked for a way to survive. I clung to a nearby tree and waited for the dawn of a new day, unsure if it was going to come.

Rescuers, helicopters, and reporters landed in the sun's rays. My people had been burned alive by the very same monster who had given us beauty, abundance, and so much life. That fateful Wednesday, rife with power and vengeance, the volcano erased our town from the face of the earth, like a misspelled word from a piece of paper.

Possessed

Things have a life of their own, it's
simply a matter of waking up
their souls.

"One Hundred Years of Solitude"

Gabriel Garcia Marquez

I was not yet aware of his presence. I enjoyed my leisure time hanging around the back garden, occupying my dull drowsiness in talking to plants, marveling about the perception, vitality and nobility we humans share with them. The gentle company of my only friends the plants, made sense of my routine. One day though, an intruder entered my state of inertia, I saw him for the first time that morning near the Canal. It was Sunday, a very sunny day. I was in the mist of watering the plants, I stopped suddenly and curiously. I sensed that he was smiling at me; his gaze was deep and fixed, static.

He saw me with his big, penetrating and wrinkled eyes; I looked back at him curiously. I immediately hid and pretended to water my plants so as not to attract his attention. I didn't want to scare him; I liked feeling observed by him. His enigmatic presence suddenly occupied my thoughts. My pulse increased; I wanted to talk to him, tell him that he was not in danger, that everything was fine; but I didn't. I thought it would be better this way, not too intimidating, not allowing contact. The nature of relationships is a mystery that can be dangerous.

Next morning, I got up expecting his return visit. As I gazed through the window overlooking the murky canal. I could hear his heavy steps, slow movements sipping of history, full of hunger and survival. Fear is the most primitive of human emotions "so they say". However, in my case it did not apply because I identified with his wild personality, his fight for his own habitat and the terrible heaviness of his body. Looking at him from a distance I found a strange pleasure in taking a close look at his features, so unique and yet, so unfamiliar.

I went quickly out to the courtyard; he walked slowly, he rested his eyes on me and magically stretched his huge jaw in front of my transfixed stare, I did not back away. Unperturbed he perched very close to the sitting area at the entrance to the courtyard. He had never dared to come so close before; and I liked even more the boldness that was so reptilian.

Thus, he remained in total stillness for a long time. I took advantage and decided to move a little closer; I saw something that he had hanging in the corner of his intimidating jaw. It was a piece of old rotting meat. I don't know why, but I immediately thought of the brain tissue that links this predator to intelligence, memory, and consciousness. He made no noise, getting closer and closer and more static; he was getting familiar.

Captivated by his enigmatic sagacity and nature, his brutal size and wisdom, I paid my full attention to his visits. I recognized him as violent and rapacious, and those were precisely the traits that brought me closer to him. I found a twisted satisfaction in being dominated by that binocular and penetrating gaze. Sadly, solitude devours the depths of hermit souls.

I approached with millimeter-close steps, wanting to touch him to let him know that I was no danger. He moved subtly, enough to give me the reassurance of getting even closer to his body. I stopped at a relevant distance, wondering how it would feel to be enveloped in the hardness of his skin. With the distance between us diminishing, the palpitations increased, and I felt them in my throat. My skin, wet with sweat took on a pale greenish color. Right there my mutation began, my blood pressure rose, and my dry tongue licked my lips. I then extended my arm almost touching the contracted muscles. I was experiencing his rigid and scaly skin. We were so close to each other that any movement would finalized the unity of the two of us, and so it did.

The density of his breath paralyzed my body; it was as if, suddenly, my will had vanished. There was no truce, no fight; we were already one. Now my body, nailed to his, finally clamped against his rough, fierce skin. I heard a sharp hiss in my brain that froze my thoughts; I heard his lungs breathe with victory, I felt my body dance uncontrollably until I finally found myself at rest.

Now my penetrating and rough eyes absorbed the ancient survival of the reptiles. My skin with rigid scales smelled of sulfur, my voice emitted an imperceptible and vague sound that did not let me breathe. I felt possessed in an ethereal way and simply merged into his nature.

In the backyard, in front of the canal, he and I, in the same being, would drag ourselves towards the water, in a state of rest. There immobile, we would gulp down the food and then push it towards our stomach. We have found that relational links are a mystery, both dangerous and fascinating.

"Chimeras"

Encounter

Someday, somewhere - anywhere,
unfailingly, you'll find yourself,
and that, and only that, can be the
happiest or bitterest hour of
your life.

Pablo Neruda

The fall

Crista, you are walking at a fast pace, almost running. You are the kind of woman who allows herself to be late for almost everything; something usually gets in the way of time and the everyday chores. Your hair is loosely tied up in a ponytail, strands of hair sprout from your temples like tangled threads that reveal whitish scales on your scalp, as well as bare areas due to lack of hair. Your body moves synchronously with the rush, your right arm digs into your bag at full speed to remove the napkin where you had written down the address, while your eyes see the pieces of broken asphalt that make a hole in the platform, forcing you to jump almost on top of the magazine stand on the right side of the sidewalk. You want to dodge it, but your poor reflexes topple you to the ground, and you knock over a good portion of the magazines. There you go Crista.

Meeting the Angelologist

Rinnng... Rinng...

"Oh, I'm coming!" This doorbell sets my nerves on edge! Hi, Crista, come in and have a seat. Sorry, something's wrong with that doorbell".

"Okay, let's see. Tell me your concerns."

"Like this... cold? I would like to feel less lost; I do not enjoy anything or anyone, I am intolerant and irascible. Sometimes I am the person I hate the most on the face of the earth. I do not understand why I am so hostile to those closest to me!"

"I understand. Look dear, in the theology of angels we are going to divide your existence and impart each segment with certain powers. You are going to be able to ease your doubts and fears. You will find the answers you seek about your existence. Here in your finite plane of reality you will find yourself softly soaring, like the wings of the most privileged and glorious beings. Your spirituality will find its roots and its heavenly source."

"Um... heavenly source? But I don't feel worthy of special planes. I don't know. I am not comfortable. What if I don't like the influence of the angels?"

"You don't have to do anything; the angels will guide you. They have been here since the beginning of creation. Crista, what are you doing to yourself? Remember what you have read about the angel Sariel and what he offers you as an alternative."

"What? Nothing with him, don't start. Just stop right there. You've clarified nothing."

"Surrender: stop playing truth and lies. Listen to the doctrine we espouse. The idea is to regulate the frequency of the waves of mental noise. You had already decided. You know it, Crista, and yet you distrust."

You can't do this to yourself Crista! This is driving you crazy... what if you just don't find your destiny here? You better go now!

"No... no. I ll talk to my life coach before I call you again, okay? I'm really not sure that your angels can answer my questions about life."

"Okay... okay. Your divinity will guide you. Take all the time you want. But I would like you to go first with the shaman and participate in a healing ritual in a trance state. You are definitely going to connect with yourself and with the Mother of all Mothers. Do you like the idea?"

"Yeah, yeah, of course. I'll try to go during the week. Bye, bye."

Meeting the Shaman

"Excuse me, may I come in?"

"No. Do not approach. Don't take a seat yet. Stand there, so I can first purify your body with an herbal rattle."

Oh God, Crista, what are you getting into? Herbal rattle? Really? Look no more at this man; he seems demented. That happens to you because you are so gullible. Crista, Crista...

"Be still woman. It will enter your body and confront the spirit that brings you into conflict. Thus the vibes of the universe will connect you with your own spirit."

"But I...."

"Silence! You are in an empty and inert plane, I sense a heavy energy from you. Chew this while getting into the same vibration as your spirit."

"Wait a minute! Can you explain to me first how this will work? Why do I have to chew these leaves? What exactly are they?"

"Shh, Shh..., I see you have a very punishing and toxic spirit. Accept the possibilities and release your being to the gods of nature, especially the spirit of Mother Ayahuasca. She may heal you with her wisdom and show you what you have to do with it, don't worry about anything, I'll lead you. The Amazonian worldview has its own soul and releases the mists of the earth and spirits. Let your inner being fly away. Do not resist it."

"But how? How? What are you throwing at me? Do you expect me to just follow your orders blindly? I just wanted you to help me with my problem."

Crista, please grab your purse and run before this guy ....

"Thank you, but I'm leaving now!"

"Don't go, Crista, the result of your search is about to be potentiated, and you are going to embark on a journey, hand in hand, with the power of the jungle. When you return, everything will make more sense. I find you very hesitant. If you think this is not what you are looking for, you are free to leave. But remember, your spirit is restless, and I think you must find it somewhere. Don't run away from your true self! Take this card and find this person when you are ready for growth. Good luck."

"Sorry, thanks anyway."

C'mon, Crista, why did you apologize to him? And why did you thank him? Oh sure, Crista, thanks for scaring me and reminding me of my awkward ignorance.

Meeting the Luminaries

"Hi Crista." Have a seat. Do you want some coffee?"

"No. No, thank you. I don't drink coffee."

"Tell me, what stars bring you here?"

"I don't know much about stars and zodiac signs, but I want to know if you can help me."

Tell her that you are confused, Crista, and anxious about your behavior. Tell her that you hurt your loved ones, and you are more and more alone. Tell her that people can no longer put up with you, that you lost your job, that you fight a lot and that you are so angry that you answer everyone rudely and aggressively. Or better yet do not tell her anything yet. Let her speak.

"Let's see what alignment the stars have with your destiny, Crista. I can give you an accurate astrological prediction, so you know how the stars see your situation, and what the future holds for you according to the rotation of the planets at the exact moment of your beautiful birth. Do you know that there are four types of elements: fire, earth, air and water? Some planets are called generational, this is because they spend years in the same sign. It may be that Neptune has stayed a long time in yours. Ah, I see that you are air, but you want to be more stable, still, and safe."

Ugh, it's hot in here!

"I understand that you want to tell me about what you know; I do understand that, and I appreciate it, but it is not what I am looking for. No, not at all. Here is the money for the session. Thank you very much."

Really? This thing about the stars, the signs and the elements... seriously, Crista? What do they have to do with your stubbornness and arrogance? You really are very frustrated, you should see someone first. Someone you haven't asked for an appointment with yet.

Meeting the Self

It has cost a lot to finally open this door, Crista. I wish I had come to you first. I know that it took me too long. I also know that I have avoided seeing you, face to face. I think the fear and shame of meeting you have delayed our meeting.

It is not so bad that it did not happen until today. I was giving you time to realize that, in the end, this visit was inevitable. Take it as the beginning of a new way of looking at life and its circumstances. What you have thought of yourself so far is a way of defending your opinion about what you want to be. It does not really represent who you are. Each conflict that you access is one face of your own nature. You take refuge in the argument to justify yourself because you are angry with your own essence and the expectation that you had about yourself.

Oh my, I'm so tired of feeling so heavy; my inner anger has led me to be cruel and neurotic. As a girl I had to be so quiet and silence my voice so much that now, as an adult, I want to shout everything at everyone. Duty was the top priority in my childhood. While the spirit of pleasure was diminished, trampling my natural instinct to please and enjoy myself. This makes me sad, and I don't know what to do with this feeling.

Reconcile with the person you are Crista. In order to heal, you must understand the disease. Self-knowledge will lead you to love yourself, without prejudice, without precepts, without attachments. Dedicate yourself to the knowledge of the "I am". That itself will give you the value of introspection towards the experience of the "here and now". Get out there and breathe love and acceptance. There is nothing you can do to make the world the way you want it to be; however, you can be the best person for that world you want.

You will be your own world. There is a lot you can do to rebuild that person you love. Pause your thinking and activate your intuition. Allow yourself to feel nothing. Smell the wind and rest. Embrace this new reality of yours.

Crista, you are tired, but there is no hurry anymore, nor is there a fight against time. Recognize your space and drop onto the plush sofa. Leave that door open. This is the last visit, but the most important. Close your eyes and finally rest.

Illusions

I am what survives of me.

Erik Erikson

Sitting in an easy chair in her room, Elena listened to a song that reminded her of a terrorizing and vicious chapter in her life that she had closed not long ago. Although distant, it rested in her mind like the story of a wild nightmare, a canvas of the past, finite, finished. She turned off the radio, canceled the intrusive memories, and got up from her chair.

 For a second she reflected on her thoughts of the close and harmful bond she had with Ariel. But she felt it was time to prove to herself that this chapter was a thing of the past. She looked at her cheap watch; the object said ten minutes to nine. "The night is young", she thought and quickly looked for something sensual to wear and some makeup to start her on the adventure.

She quickly checked her handbag, counted one by one the objects she needed: money, lipstick, keys, mints, condom, and identification. She lowered her tight pants to her hips and ruffled her hair to gain volume and seduction.

As she drove to the selected disco, she enjoyed, with a smile, the freedom that she had allowed to herself that night. In her veins, the blood ran with speed and frenzy as she, in her mind, imagined, from beginning to end, the outcome of a nocturnal encounter of passion and madness.

In the darkness of the disco, the music exceeded the decibels suitable for meaningful communication. Hundreds of figures, dancing closely with curved, slow, and seductive movements, brought each skin, each scent, each smile closer together. Moving seductively from the center of the dance floor, she saw a male figure approaching. A flurry of palpitations warned her that it was time to be vigilant, to be ready; She hadn't felt something like that for many years. Stalking the man, Elena felt the euphoric tingle of her skin. She did not know him; and it made her burn with pleasure. As she danced with slow movements towards her target, she looked at him with the thirst with which an addict assesses his drug. She approached his tall, well-built body. They danced so close that he could smell her sweat, feel her vibration, hear her silent invitation. He took her by the shoulders, turned and pressed her tightly to his chest, clasped their hands and rested them on her breasts. Her nipples tightened as he moved her to the rhythm of electronic music. Drunk with eroticism, she surrendered to his sensory commands, their interlocking hands lowered. She inhaled deeply into her belly, and a torrent of blood reached her brain. She no longer could listen to the music; she only felt the sensation of pleasure in her entrails, in the depths of her stomach. The man could also hear his own muffled moans become more audible. The intimate stranger's hands found their way, and seductively, dance over her abdomen. From behind, she felt his robust and erect member. Her vulnerability escalated, and fragile, she was slowly fading with pleasure and ecstasy. He, without announcing and with audacious performance, leveled Elena's pants with his hands, sliding them slowly, provoking her with his fierce and visceral sexuality. She then found herself in a warm and thick ocean, succumbing to the intimate adventure, expanding her femininity, her intimacy. Elena's mouth parted with a groan as his fingers danced lustfully and playfully on her pelvis. Their bodies, adhered by the music and the pleasure of the night, fiercely lost themselves in an uncontrollable sea of sensations. There were no witnesses; there were no objects; there were no labels; there were no plans for the future. They were in a dimension where only the two of them could exist in a universal constant. The rest of the world was turned off. They were absorbed by a great black hole that rotated in hyperspace: where music, voices and the presence of a place were heard less and less.

The next day, Elena woke up triumphant in her bed. A shaft of light came through the ajar window. She sat up with her back straight and stretched her arms towards infinity. Then she opened them widely and left them up in the air as if expanding her chest to put all the oxygen in the universe in a single inhalation.

She thought of calling her sister and telling her this beautiful experience. She stopped for a moment and imagined her sister asking: "But do you know him? Is he for real, does he work? Did he agree to something? Or are you going to continue the same cycle...?"

Convinced that the present time is always better, she closed her eyes and smiled gratefully: stripped of all expectations, satisfied.

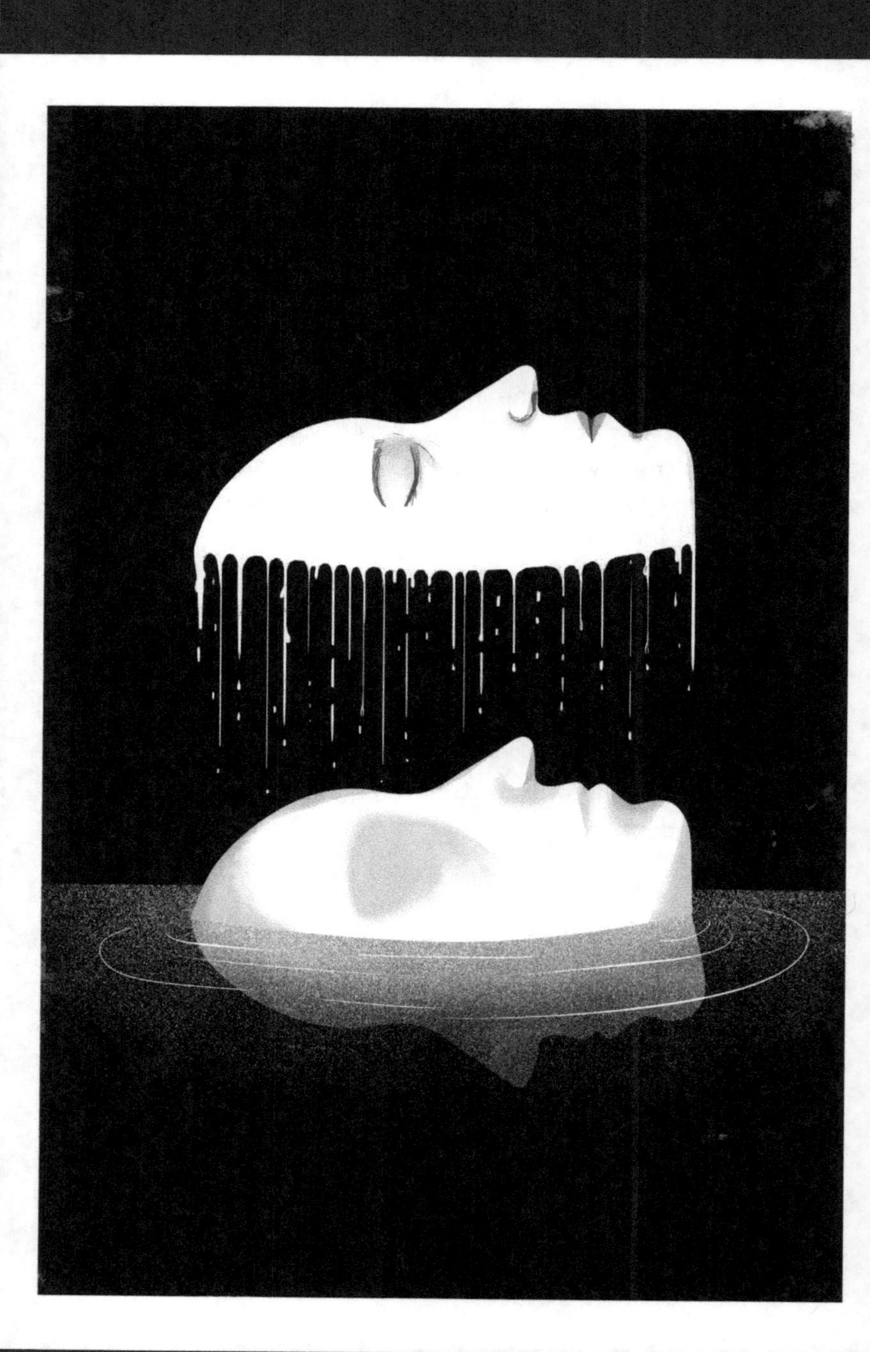

Lost
Identity

I awake from a deep sleep to find that I am not still in the hospital bed injured and unconscious. I begin to remember.

The place is narrow, padded with a soft fabric like satin. It's totally dark with no ventilation. My cold, immobile body finally finds loneliness; it doesn't scare me. I think that Irene, at last, has listened to my pleas, I will no longer have to endure this life which I have dragged myself through.

Many voices approach that are indistinguishable. I hear one in particular that begins to cry: it is my mother. She regrets with guilt my absence. She apologizes for her negligence in my upbringing. With her I remember my childhood, my adolescence, the times I ran away from school, the times I stole money from her to buy a friend a beer. I remember the nights that I did not come home to sleep, and I left her full of worry and anguish. Her short steps are heard moving quietly into the distance.

A male voice lifts me out of regrets. It's Jorge, my first boy-friend; he doesn't cry, he just speaks in a slow tone, almost whispers.

"Lila, my love, I can't believe you're not with us anymore. What happened? I told you that I would always be there for you, that I would always be waiting for your call. I'm sorry I didn't kiss you tenderly one last time. You know you were my only love."

Hearing it, my heart trembles. I always wanted to look for him and apologize for having slept with his best friend: I know that tore him apart. We were very young, I have never felt more ashamed than that day when Jorge opened the bathroom door at his parents' house and caught us. I felt very bad when, as a result of anger, he left school and did not want to be part of the group anymore: he annulled himself from us, who were his only friends. Hearing his words fills me with tranquility and peace. Lost in my thoughts, I do not realize that is gone, but it is already another voice that speaks to me, very close to the wall of my confinement.

"Mija, you always concerned me with the nonsense of not talking about your issues, always so quiet, suffering alone. What happened, my baby? You should have called me; you should have come to see me. You knew that I was never going to judge you for anything. Your departure hurts a lot. Sudden-ly, I feel that I should have looked for you more, to be present in your pain. Now I understand that it was not your arrogance; you simply did not know how to ask for help. I love you very much, little one. May God keep you in his love and forgive you unconditionally."

She is my Aunt Carol, I thought she hated me with her soul full of hollow religious conventions. I hear footsteps, many more footsteps. They move away and come closer. I don't know what's going on out there. I feel cold, and my head is spinning. However, I am calm; my palpitations are slow and rhythmic. Hearing the voices of those close to me and knowing what they thought about me is really refreshing. Several friends pass by. Some close friends that I don't see very often, other distant friends with whom I speak from time to time. I listen to neighbors and former teachers. Why should so many people have taken the time to come see me off?

"I don't know what to tell you flaca, it would be good to start by asking your forgiveness. but I am sure, that, from heaven or hell, or wherever you are, you are going to refute and contradict everything I tell you! I hope you did not suffer at the time of your death, I know we did not end well, but this last time you really provoked me. How is it possible that you got so drunk? You couldn't even stand up by yourself. And that man who brought you, you didn't even know him! There were many times, flaca, many things. I'm sorry I hit you while you were unconscious ... I'm so sorry for the times I hit you, the times I yelled at you, the times I ridiculed you. I'm sorry I didn't value you. When I took you to the hospital, I couldn't say I was your husband: they would have taken me to prison, flaca. That's why I left you lying there. I apologize! I never imagined that you would be able to hurt yourself. Your family and I looked for you everywhere. In the hospital they didn't realize when you left. Your family was desperate... me too. You were always so willful and rebellious. Look ... if it hadn't been for Irene who warned us, flaca, who knows what would have happened.

I can't believe what I hear. It's him. How dare he! I am paralyzed. He has decided to enter to "say goodbye." I know him so well that I always knew that he would find a way to get here, in the midst of so many people who hate him, and were so against this relationship, that they always bet on a disastrous ending. They almost got it right because he almost beat me to death.

My palpitations increase suddenly, I feel a cold sweat that soaks my back, my tears run to my temples. This visit, this last goodbye makes my blood boil. Suddenly this narrow place dressed in satin, which is now my refuge, bothers me...threatens me. It proudly warns me about the possibility of unveiling reality. I have difficulty breathing, I clasp my hands to paralyze my momentum. My chest becomes small from the need of air, I want to vomit. The space is reduced even more, and I feel strange to myself, I feel that I am floating trapped in my own body, in my own delusion.

Someone rapped upon the wood, I recognize the voice, it is Irene. She is angry.

"I already saw the asshole. Shameless! How did he get in? Everything will be fine. Hang on friend; I'm here for you, we're in this together. Don't you let him get away with it, hang on."

I have to trust her. Irene is right, she knows I'm desperate.

Abruptly they lift my hiding place: now the coffin rocks from side to side. My head is spinning. Finally, they place me on a flat surface. I can't wait for the funeral home to close. I can't wait for this whole charade to end. Irene calms me down. She speaks to me in code, tells me that in a few minutes my heaven will open. I will see the fruit of salvation.

I'm not sure. As always, I realize too late that I have stepped into this funnel myself: now that I hear what everyone thinks of me, now that I see that they are sorry, now that they value me, now that I feel appreciated... But now, without my life, I realize that I had always had the opportunity to live in the best way, but I never wanted to take the reins. And now it is too late.

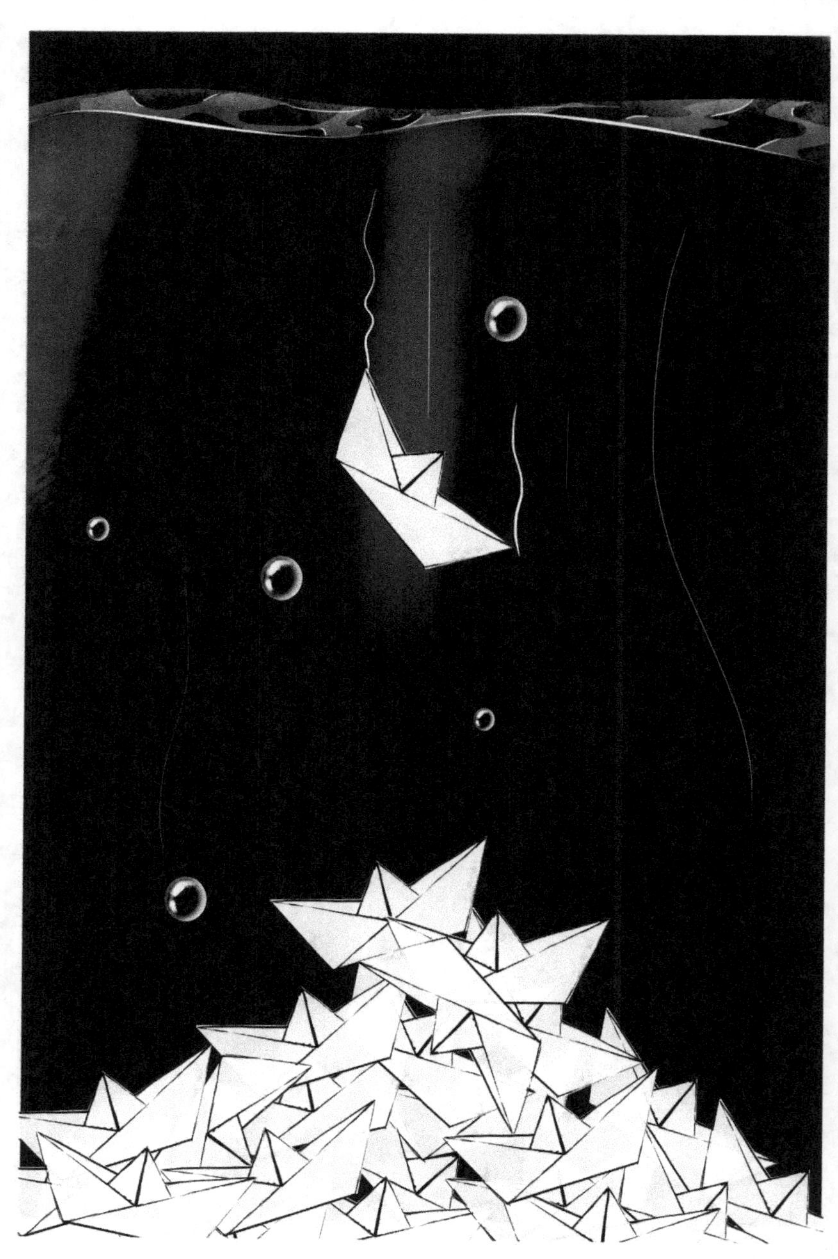

Paper Boats

It is by separating when you feel and
understand the strength with which
you love yourself.

Fyodor Dostoevsky

The most exciting moment was when everything was ready: cold cuts, soda, wood for the stove, plastic plates and glasses, and an old soccer ball to play "Passing the ball". All of us ran and huddled our bodies together, full of joy for the day ahead. For our mother and us, these open-air lunches were "The great Adventure" once a month on Sundays. For her, they were the maternal gift of love for her children: adventure and joy in the river.

We mounted everything onto truck that my mother had rented to take us in the morning and pick us up in the afternoon. She took the opportunity to wash this month's dirty clothes for us. While she was laundering in the river, we children organized the rest: the bonfire, the clotheslines, the blankets to sit down to eat. Each group had something to do. First, we built a puddle pool with stones for the little ones, so that they could play there until they were wrinkled like raisins.

We, older siblings, took care of the food while we entertained ourselves by telling jokes and clowning around to amuse my mother, who was beating the blankets on the stones so that, according to her, they would be cleaner. Every now and then, we would keep an eye on the little ones to make sure they were safe and didn't get out of the puddle. But that Sunday, the Pance River would deliver an unexpected blow to us.

Nestor's inner voice began, "This was what happened. My younger brothers and I played in the river pool. Fermin, as he was the oldest, had told us that if we wanted something, we should yell at him, and that for nothing in the world should we jump off the stones. But when the little paper boat escaped from the rocks, I looked at Alba. She said something to me, but I couldn't hear her because the river was making a lot of noise. With that, she pulled my hair towards her and that hurt a lot. It also made me angry. I took her hand off my head and told her to leave me alone, and that I just wanted to reach my little, blue paper boat. Alba didn't care. She was just saying to listen to her because it was dangerous. I looked over to where my mom was washing, but she couldn't even see us from her vantage point. My older brothers had the music blaring and were laughing out loud, so I tried to reach my little boat holding onto one of the stones.

Alba, barely ten years old, tried to help me by pulling my shirt from behind. I stretched my arm, but the stone moved and made me lose my balance. My skinny body slid between the stones and within the pull of the river current. Alba could not hold me anymore. I felt a stream of water enter my mouth, and my heart began to beat faster and louder. Suddenly, I felt a hard blow on my back. The image of my mother crossed my mind. I knew the current was carrying me. I desperately wanted to hang onto the tree branches that hung on the shore, but my hands were sliding through the swampy mud. When I tried to lift my head out of the water, my body would slide between one stone and another, and I could no longer control it. I raised my arm as my mom had taught us, but the current was so strong that my head was hitting the stones. For a brief moment, in the distance I could see my little paper boat. I wanted to cry, but since my eyes were under water, I didn't feel the tears. I kept swallowing water until I wanted to vomit, and I no longer felt the struggle. My body was very heavy. I gave up."

When my little brother died, none of us older siblings imagined that in the loneliness of Nestor's absence, we would also lose our mother. She, who was always the spirit of the meetings, was also emotionally gone. It had been a Sunday in June, and the last river outing we ever had. That was five years ago, and not a day goes by without guilt reminding us of the rush of the water and the unpredictability of a child's behavior in the quest for a desired object.

That loss changed our mother. She worked, came and went, cooked, went to the store, bought the groceries, returned home, stared blankly from the balcony, watered the plants, scrubbed the front of the house, checked some corner, made the beds, refreshed a vase, made a call or cried a ballad. She went through all the motions. Late at night we heard her whisper a song: "Children don't die; they go to heaven. They stay in our souls and put on wings, and they fly very close. Children do not die. They go for a time to gather stars and are born again in another little one."

I suffered when I saw her pain, I wanted to read her soul, to be able to heal and console her as Starets Zósima did with the woman who lost her little son in *The Karamázov Brothers.*

A few days ago, our mother went out in the morning to visit a neighbor who was ill in the hospital. When she returned, she was carrying in her arms a bundle full of her friend's clothes. She told us it was for washing. It was strange because since little Nestor's death, she did not wash again. She always asked one of us to wash her clothes.

We celebrated for this sudden act of generosity. She returned to being herself, and that day resumed normal activities without damaged emotions on display. But the next day, she didn't come out anymore. She didn't even open the door to her room. From within and with a hushed voice, she answered that she was fine and that we should continue making dinner without her. She would catch up with us later.

We heard the song "Children do not die, they go for a time to gather stars and are born again in another little one."

That night she did not come out for dinner. At dawn I heard her murmuring "Shh...shh", but I didn't say anything.

It was six thirty in the morning when a piteous infant cry woke us up suddenly, we ran alarmed, to my mother's room. The door was locked and barred:

"Mom, please open the door"!

"What happened? We're fine. Go back to sleep!" she answered in a nervous voice.

"Mom, please! Why is there a baby with you?"

"Don't make noise, you're scaring him. Leave us alone. In a little while your little brother will calm down. Hush, hush...shh."

The baby kept crying; it was a high-pitched and strident cry, like a scream. We were really worried and did not know what to do. A thousand frantic questions came to our minds.

"Whose baby is that? Where did she get it? How is she feeding it? Why would she have brought a baby home?"

An hour later, our house was the epicenter of the neighborhood. Crowded at the entrance were the police, the hospital staff and the neighbors. The latter were curious and wanting to know what had happened to our mother that would result in such an unacceptable act of madness.

When we entered my mother's room, the first thing we could see was a collection of paper boats of various sizes, colors and models. Behind them stood our mother grasping a baby and a blue paper boat.

End

Instinto

cuentos cortos

Instinto

cuentos cortos

Vivi Merrill

Instinto: Cuentos cortos
© Vivi Merrill
Primera edición, 2021

Diseño de portada e ilustraciones
Isabella Manjarrés Melo @imailustracion
Diagramación
Hugo H. Ordóñez Nievas

———————————

Sugerencias y comentarios
vivimerrill.usa@gmail.com

Redes sociales

vivimerrill

———————————

Asesoría editorial

Este libro, o parte de él, no puede ser reproducido por ningún medio sin autorización escrita del titular de los derechos correspondientes.

Impreso en México
Diciembre, 2021

Reconocer y aceptar mi
propia insensatez me acerca a
la cordura de otros...
que somos todos.

Acerca de los cuentos

¿Se pueden poner en las manos del lector historias de ficción que aluden a su propia historia, la de un vecino, la de un amigo? Esa es precisamente la cuestión en estas doce narraciones. El libro es una invitación a reflexionar a través de una mirada que siente, que observa y escruta la anomalía y el desasosiego como designios aparentemente irrenunciables en la vida cotidiana, que bien puede ser la de cualquiera de nosotros. Una mujer engullida por la soledad, una adolescente que ávida de aventura halla su último suspiro en manos de un desconocido, una madre atrapada en un duelo desgarrador por la muerte de su pequeño, la mente de un hombre enclaustrada en su infancia, y otros relatos breves sobre el fenómeno del universo cotidiano, son sombras de un horizonte social que invitan a entrar en el complejo mundo de otros seres humanos.

Instinto es un libro que pretende despertar en el lector el mundo psicológico del *yo*, que somos todos, pretende invitarlo a la comprensión de lo cotidiano en los otros. Reconocer esa constante de la búsqueda del espíritu humano y sus avatares, es un desafío. Como dice el maestro Octavio Paz: "Para que pueda ser he de ser otro, salir de mí, buscarme entre los otros, los otros que no son si yo no existo, los otros que me dan plena existencia."

A través de estos cuentos cortos, el lector va a incursionar en el mundo de cada uno de los personajes. La fragilidad, el riesgo, la locura y la mente alienada son algunos escenarios de una lectura llena de angustia y realidad.

En mi práctica psicoterapéutica he encontrado seres humanos que conviven con una enfermedad, con un trastorno mental, con la pérdida de alguien amado, con un vacío que no le da sentido a su existir o con un conflicto irresoluble. Esas experiencias, escondidas detrás de la máscara de lo cotidiano, afloran a través la literatura y vienen a desestabilizar el inconsciente colectivo.

A todos los que sufren
mi inquietud literaria.

Cuentos

"La voz interna de lo distinto"

La
hazaña

Únicamente aquello que nunca deja
de doler se queda en la memoria.

Michel Foucault

Pensó que iba en un vehículo porque su cuerpo giraba y se golpeaba violentamente: contra la espalda, en la cabeza, en las costillas y ¡zas! volvía a la posición central. La sensación de la cinta adhesiva en la boca lo desesperaba. Perdía la esperanza de que alguien viniera en su auxilio.

Se retorcía con ímpetu. Los brazos no los podía mover, al tratar de hacerlo se revolcaba como las larvas. Pensó en cómo comenzó su día, trató de recordar si había dejado los huevos en la estufa... Otra vuelta brusca del vehículo, otro golpe en la cabeza; otra vez el dolor.

Algo olía fétido, se paralizó para concentrarse en el origen de aquel olor putrefacto que le recordaba la letrina de su niñez... Eran quince personas entre hermanos, padres, primos, tíos y abuelos. Vivían en una choza de dos habitaciones a las afueras del pueblo y excretaban en un mismo pozo.

Empezó a escuchar voces indistinguibles, le costaba trabajo identificar de quienes eran; eran dos o tres. Se colaban chirridos de ruedas y gritos autoritarios. Se movió de nuevo, intentó liberarse con las piernas pues estaban libres, las encogió como en posición fetal, dio un fuerte golpe contra lo que pensó que era el centro del baúl y escuchó un estruendoso ruido metálico.

Aprovechó para arrastrarse hacia el vacío, se dio cuenta de que era su posibilidad de huir. En el intento chocó de golpe contra algo que no supo distinguir. Cayó y logró pararse rápidamente. Sintió un dolor punzante en el tobillo derecho que lo hizo cojear, sin embargo, con pasos cortos e inestables, arrancó la fuga.

Todo estaba oscuro, no obstante, lograba percibir entre sombras algunos movimientos lentos. Finalmente había logrado la hazaña de liberarse. Caminó unos pasos para saber dónde estaba, sintió una pared vieja, con huecos carcomidos por el tiempo y la apatía. Con el brazo encogido se sostuvo sobre ella, al tacto la pared se desmoronó un poco, miró al piso y advirtió que algunos bichos habían caído con la pared. Pensó nuevamente en esa mañana, en la estufa, en los huevos.

Le mortificaba haber dejado el gas prendido (los huevos se quemarían) sus pensamientos estaban cada vez más confusos.

Buscó el reloj en su muñeca para saber la hora, no lo halló. Al ver que no lo traía, advirtió que del brazo, que había tocado la pared, salía un salpullido rosáceo. Le picaba, sintió una carga atroz de calor. Ahora el salpullido era de un color marrón, parecía que cada roncha se movía bajo la piel demandando espacio para salir del brazo. Tuvo miedo, pensó en que eso podía ser una invasión y quedó paralizado. Recordó a Gregorio Samsa: ¡Si tan solo se hubiese parado de la cama a las cuatro como todas las mañanas, si tan solo se hubiera obligado a voltear su espalda para quedar en el lado derecho de la cama!

De pronto entró en una profunda preocupación y se sintió solo. Al igual que Samsa, él se perdía en las sombras de una habitación. Calculó la distancia que lo separaba de la pared a la puerta de metal. Era extremadamente lejana, inhóspita, vacía. La desesperanza lo acogió con rabia.

Detrás de su cabeza se alzaba una nube gris opaca. Volteó con desconfianza para mirar bien. Estaba seguro de que esa era otra artimaña del secuestrador: ahora quería controlar su pensamiento y sacarle información sobre la Organización Mundial de la Salud. El dolor en el tobillo lo distrajo del pensamiento, unos segundos después, escuchó que alguien intentaba abrir la puerta, se quedó inmóvil observando. Pasaron décadas de espera, le sorprendió que pudiera ver la puerta con tanta claridad. Olió a huevo, a quemado, a suciedad, corrió hacia la puerta de metal, no lograba detenerla. Alguien iba a entrar con fuego y al contacto con el gas explotaría todo. Con rapidez trataba de encontrar la perilla de seguridad, pero la puerta era lisa, solo tenía un pequeño orificio con rejas en la parte superior. No logró alcanzarlo.

Terminó sentado de rodillas sosteniendo la puerta con su espalda. No podía respirar bien, tenía los ojos extraviados y las palpitaciones ahogaban su pecho, la garganta seca se hizo un nudo. Cansado de luchar, intentó gritar. Su voz nunca salió.

Cuando entramos, Samuel se hallaba desmayado contra la puerta de la austera habitación. Se había golpeado contra las paredes hasta sangrar. La camisa de fuerza estaba roja y claramente se veían los estragos físicos de la transformación mental. Era evidente que la visita de los familiares le había producido un cúmulo de síntomas negativos. Yo se los había advertido, pero, como es sabido: ¡La porfía de los familiares es la madre de todas las crisis!

Rocco

El hombre es un ser perverso por su
naturaleza, y aunque somos seres
racionales, esta misma perversión
inhibe cualquier rastro de raciocinio
en nosotros.

"El Niño Proletario"
Osvaldo Lamborghini

Yo tenía como diez años... Recibí un perrito como premio
por haber pasado quinto nítido, sin perder ni una materia y
con más de ochenta: un gran logro. De todos los hermanos yo
era el único hijo con buenas calificaciones para las expectati-
vas de mis padres, que ya para entonces se conformaban con
que cualquier hijo pasara.

El perro llegó a casa justo la misma tarde de verano del día
de la clausura. En el pasillo de la sala, mis hermanos alegaban
sobre lo injusto del premio, pues, según ellos, yo era el más
mal portado y grosero de todos nosotros. Pero eso sí: el que
no había perdido ni una materia.

—Dejen tranquilo a Fernandito, él se ganó el derecho a su
perro y él verá qué hace con él. Ustedes aprendan a ganar-
se las cosas con su comportamiento —dijo mi madre, y nadie
chistó.

Mi mamá y yo le pusimos Rocco. Al principio me seguía por
todos los rincones, dormitaba la mayor parte del tiempo y
comía como un muerto de hambre. Como era mío, le enseñé
que yo era su amo y que me debía obedecer para evitar cas-
tigos o consecuencias. Así lo adiestré. Pasaron varios días de
entrenamientos y juegos perrunos.

Lo paseaba por el parque. Le tiraba la pelota. Jugábamos y nos hacíamos compañía. Prefería estar con él antes que con mis hermanos o con mis compañeros de la escuela. En las tardes nos íbamos de caza y perseguíamos gatos abandonados. Una vez corrimos un gato siamés, su pelo brillaba y tenía un cascabelito. Rocco lo alcanzó, lo tenía contra la pared, pero no se atrevió a morderlo. Agarré al gato a patadas para que Rocco aprendiera a ser fuerte y a hacerse respetar. El gato gimió y Rocco se escondió detrás de mí con la cola entre las patas. Enfurecido, lo castigué: lo dejé atado, sin comida y sin agua.

Pronto comencé a notar que Rocco no me dejaba solo en ningún momento y me hacía tropezar con todo: "¡Quítate, perro cobarde!", le gritaba veinte veces al día. Este perro le temía a la lluvia, al viento, a los ruidos. Empezó a molestarme mucho. Además, vivía pidiendo comida, tenía que limpiar su popó, bañarlo, y en las noches no quería dormir en su casita. ¡Uf, ya no podía soportar que se atravesara en mi camino, por su culpa yo vivía de mal humor!

Pensé entonces que debía idear un plan para acabar con esta molestia. Mis hermanos no querían ayudarme y me decían: el perrito es tuyo, pues, ¿o no?

Dejó de meterse entre mis patas, cuando le corté las uñas bien cortitas, le salió sangre. Se las bañé en alcohol para que no se fueran a infectar. De hecho, ¡le metí todas las patas en alcohol!

Maga, mi hermana menor, miraba en silencio desde el otro lado de la cocina y movía la cabeza de un lado a otro. Las lágrimas le corrían por las mejillas. Ella poco hablaba, "la rara", la llamaba yo. La ignoré. Estaba orgulloso de la forma que encontré para que el perro estuviera acostado y dejara de tropezarse conmigo por toda la casa.

Desde lo de las uñas, lloriqueaba todo el día el maldito perro. No lo soportaba. No podía cortarle la lengua pues mi mamá me hubiera matado a mí. Pero sí encontré una manera de que se callara sin que nadie supiera el porqué. El perro ya no ladraba ni lloriqueaba. No se lo conté a nadie, solo yo sabía la razón de su silencio. Emití una risita traviesa.

Las heridas se agravaban cada día más y el perro cobarde ya no se podía parar ni a orinar ni a hacer popó, así que me tocó sacarlo al patio y amarrarlo cerca de la tierra: ahí hacía todo y se arrastraba en su propia mierda. A la semana, dejó de comer, no tomaba agua y olía a podrido. ¡Perro cobarde! Fue una maldición haber sacado buenas calificaciones. Por esa razón no volví a ser buen estudiante.

—Ya es hora, Fernando, alguien más espera su turno. Ya sabe cómo es aquí —me interrumpió el psiquiatra. El guardia daba golpecitos en la reja de hierro para anunciar que ya era hora de regresar a la celda.

—Gracias doctor, me gustó el juego de contar algo de mi niñez. Esta es tan sólo una de tantas anécdotas de mi infancia. Se me ocurre la idea de escribir un libro, ya sabe doctor, ya sembré un árbol y tuve varios hijos.

Gotas
de lluvia

En el grupo éramos muy unidas, el juego de canasta tenía lugar todas las tardes en casa de una de nosotras, nos turnábamos durante la semana.

La señora Gordillo era de la clase de mujer que se emperifollaba con joyas y tacones para salir a jugar canasta con sus amigas en el jardín de las casas. Ella era, entre todas, las más particular; siempre vestía un sombrero negro de capa angosta, de esos de los años cincuenta, según ella, porque en cualquier momento podía llover y las gotas de lluvia arruinarían su maquillaje.

Su esposo, un hombre adinerado y de poco tiempo, era muy ausente de su hogar, pues dedicaba largas jornadas de trabajo en su empresa. Nunca tuvieron hijos, ella tenía un problema en el útero, un síndrome de nombre Asherman, o algo así.

La señora Gordillo era de gustos extravagantes y divinamente espléndida. Ese día salió al supermercado para que en la tarde cuando nos sentáramos a jugar en su casa, tuviéramos vino, mazapanes, bocadillos y pastel. Pero esa tarde llovió, cayó una tempestad tremenda y la señora no pudo evitar que con tanta agua su maquillaje se arruinara. Desde mi ventana, la vi llegar. Entró despacio, con un semblante pálido y contraído, corrí a su casa para saber qué había pasado y, claro, para ofrecer mi ayuda. El juego de canasta sería esa misma tarde.

¡Que las gotas de agua se le habían metido por los poros de la cabeza! Eso sostuvo. Lloraba desconsoladamente mientras sacudía la cabeza con fuerza, daba saltitos con una sola pierna, primero la derecha, después la izquierda.

Ya éramos tres las amigas que estábamos acompañándola. Su esposo no llegaba, la noche había caído. Su compostura se había transformado. La cara pálida, las pupilas dilatadas y el pulso muy lento describían los síntomas de un estado de pánico de alto riesgo.

En el periódico salió la noticia de un hombre que había muerto debido al tormento de una gota de agua en la coronilla. La desesperación lo volvió loco, había perdido los estribos y con ellos la vida. Eso fue lo que empeoró la creencia de la señora Gordillo, que suponía que las gotas de lluvia podían inundarle el cerebro. Ella siempre argumentaba que era su maquillaje, sin embargo, lo que temía era que el cerebro se le ahogara.

Estábamos preocupadas, todas acompañándola como buenas amigas. Lo primero que hicimos fue conectar un drenaje que llegara al oído y saliera a una cubeta en el piso, lo cual no funcionó porque escasamente salió media gota de lluvia.

Yo tuve la idea de ponerle un casco de espuma y dejarle la cabeza colgando en la cama por un rato. Ese método sí dio resultado, la espuma se mojó y todas vimos una mejoría en la expresión de la señora Gordillo.

No hablaba, los ojos no le funcionaban, la piel ya estaba tomando el tono del agua encharcada y el esposo no llegaba. La situación era desesperante. Cayendo la madrugada, vi cómo sus ojos medio se movieron, del fondo de la garganta salió un leve ronquido, muy agudo. Me acerqué con miedo, al verla tan mal ahí mismo tomé la decisión, no podíamos esperar más por el esposo: ¡había que hacer algo!

Entre tres de nosotras, la atamos a la cama, para que con la molestia del procedimiento no se moviera. Alistamos el material, el medicamento y nos encomendamos al espíritu de los milagros, a la madre de todos los santos y a la divinidad de la naturaleza.

Cuando la manguera entró por el canal auditivo, tuvimos que sostenerla aún más fuerte. Empujamos con fuerza la sonda para poder romper la membrana timpánica, la pasamos de extremo a extremo por el conducto frontonasal y ahí lo detuvimos para que absorbiera el agua que había entrado por los poros de la cabeza. Estaba funcionando muy bien. Ante los ojos de todas nosotras, la palidez tomaba un color diferente, algo así como un verde pálido, pero se veía mejor. De repente, sus ojos comenzaron a moverse en todas las direcciones, el cuerpo se erguía como dándonos señales de que ya casi salía toda el agua. Ella estaba cooperando. Nosotras le sosteníamos cabeza, cuerpo y extremidades. La cubeta se iba llenando de agua, ya no parecía de lluvia, pero al fin de cuentas había pasado por su cuerpo y eso le daba un color rojizo suave. Ya la señora Gordillo no estaba tan rígida, por el contrario, su cuerpo poco a poco fue cediendo.

Cuando el movimiento cesó, nos sentimos más aliviadas, olía un poco a ácido, como a formol, pero el poderla ayudar nos reconfortó. A los primeros cantos del gallo, una a una salimos para nuestras casas, la dejamos descansar, se veía inmóvil y en paz, yo fui la última en salir. Su esposo fue el primero que la encontró en su nuevo estadio.

La
bestia

Los animales son de Dios.
La bestialidad es humana.

Víctor Hugo

Te encontré en la blancura de la mañana, ahí en esa tiendita, sentada con cara de querer. Te invité a caminar por el parque y aceptaste. Hasta siempre te daré las gracias.

Caminamos un rato, con tu carita preocupada me contaste que no habías ido a la escuela, que ese día estabas de humor para algo más. Yo, entonces, oportunista, quise capturar tu mente y hacerme tu amigo.

Llegamos al parque cerca de la catedral, donde los sauces guardan secretos y los novios se encuentran a jugar travesuras. Pero nosotros no éramos novios y tú no sabías jugar travesuras. Te tiré a la hierba, recuerdo tu mirada de sorpresa. Para mi ventaja, el viento deslizó con fuerza tu cabello largo a la boca y a los ojos, ya no hablabas, ya no veías.

Un hilo de sangre salió de tu vulva y tu piel se demacró. Tus ojos apretados lloraban en silencio, ya no supe si por dolor o por pasión pueril. Quisiste moverte, pero el peso de mi cuerpo te lo impidió. Ya mi piel bajo tus uñas, ya mi aliento dentro de tus venas.

Entre dientes murmurabas algo, no estoy seguro si de la escuela o de tu bicicleta, callé tus quejidos con mis manos. Tu mirada palideció, tus piernas quedaron inmóviles. Mis manos siempre estarán impresas en tu blanco y lánguido cuello. Abandonada, tu alma quedó entre dos sauces. Satisfecho, devolví mis ojos para verte una última vez; ya sin pulso tus labios oscurecidos no llamaron mi atención.

A lo lejos vi humo, te escondí entre ramas; era humo negro. Nadie nos vio, en el parque de los sauces nadie nos vio. Quedaste inerte en la nada.

"Desde el Yo"

La espera

Cuando mis ojos se abrieron, miré el reloj: eran las cuatro y media de la mañana. A mi edad esta rutina era cada vez más normal. Estiré el brazo para alcanzar el agua que estaba en la mesita de noche, torpemente tumbé el vaso al piso. Asustada, traté de pararme más rápido pero no lo logré. Debía ser cuidadosa y no exponerme a accidentes, mis huesos ya no aguantarían una caída más. El día prometía ser especial, pues vería al único hombre que me escuchaba y empaticamente aceptaba mis achaques, mi insuficiencia emotiva y mis quejas. Todo un mes guardé la esperanza de hablar con él, el día estaba frente a mí. Con lentitud y cuidado esquivé el vaso roto y salí a la cocina a preparar mi té.

Me recogí el cabello. En las mañanas me da náuseas el olor que expulsa, es un olor a grasa y sudor, revuelto con el pachulí que rocío en la almohada para dormir por lo menos unas horas de corrido. Me duché, me eché talco en el cuerpo y terminé el té.

Para las seis de la mañana ya estaba lista, con mi vestido blanco de encaje de hilo, que tanto critica mi hijo, especialmente cuando su visión doble, alcoholizada, lo confunde con una pijama o batón de baño y vocifera que no sea una madre irrespetuosa y exhibicionista, pero con todo y eso, es mi vestido favorito.

Me senté en la banca de madera rústica que está al lado de la chimenea, despacio me recosté en el respaldo y, como si estuviera jugando a los "congelados", no volví a mover un dedo voluntariamente. Esperé, esperé y esperé sin tomar ni una gota de agua hasta un poco antes de las dos de la tarde, hora en que lo veía.

La cita era siempre la misma, a la hora en punto y con idéntica rutina. Yo esperaba ansiosa este día, porque para mí era un alivio, un respiro enorme de oxígeno. Le tenía que contar que me había caído y tuve que esperar a mi hijo porque no podía levantarme. Pero cuando llegó, estaba tan borracho que tropezó con la lámpara de cristal, que por tantos años yo había cuidado esmeradamente, era un regalo de mi amado difunto. Mi hijo vomitó en el piso, creí que se tragaría el vómito porque hiperventilaba mientras tosía y tosía. Mis gritos pidiendo ayuda eran tan fuertes que a mi vecina no le quedó más remedio que llegar en mi apoyo.

Una vez en la oficina, la secretaria me hizo sentar en un sofá acolchonado y moderno, de esos que decoran las casas de los magazines. Me ofreció una revista *Vogue*.

–Para que se distraiga –dijo.

Yo no la acepté, en este punto ya no era una espera, era ansiedad y miedo de olvidar algo. Esperé veinte minutos antes de verlo, me saludó atentamente, con voz firme, pero empática, afable.

–¿Hola Anna, cómo se ha sentido este último mes? ¿Cómo van las cosas con su hijo?

Yo lo miré y, con voz dubitativa y temblorosa, comencé a hablar. Hablé de mí, de mis soledades, de las ausencias nocturnas tan grandes que el vacío de mi esposo dejaba, hablé de las largas noches en las que planeaba mi encuentro con él, y también hablé de cómo lo soñaba. Le conté que mi piel arrugada sentía la resequedad del viento en el otoño.

Entonces, de vez en cuando paraba para ver su cara, su expresión, como si de alguna manera esperara su aprobación para seguir hablando. Él decía: continúa mujer, continúa. Y acto seguido escribía en su computadora. A veces abría un pequeño libro de bolsillo y dibujaba. Continúa Anna, continúa; decía. Yo tuve tiempo para acordarme de una cuñada que murió hace mucho. Entre llanto y llanto hablé del dolor de perder a mi hijo en vida o, mejor aún, de su perdida vida en el alcohol y de la angustia que me daba no poder caminar a mi perro Miki... Hablé, hablé y hablé sin parar pero no le conté que me había caído: me olvidé de todo lo que había planeado decirle.

Ah, y no hizo falta contarle sobre cómo avanza el problema de mi vejiga ni decirle que el pachulí ya no sirve para nada porque justo cuando estaba a punto de contarle, él miró el reloj que estaba estratégicamente puesto sobre la mesita auxiliar consigo al sofá. Volteó su mirada haca mí y rápidamente notó mi vestido empapado y, en el diván, un gran círculo oscuro que revelaba mi problema.

Él cerró su computadora y dijo: ya es tiempo Anna, debemos parar aquí.

Salí en silencio,caminando sola con mis pensamientos y tan avergonzada...

Desde
mis ojos

El único castigo que tuve en mi existencia ocurrió en un día que comenzó común y corriente. Reinaban la calma y la paz, que son el regalo más extraordinario de la naturaleza. Hacía muy poco tiempo que habíamos llegado a vivir a Tamarón, una ciudad donde los ciudadanos aman a sus mascotas.

Recuerdo bien ese día, eran como las nueve, yo ya había salido a caminar con mi mamá y también había desayunado. La mañana estaba fresca, los árboles bailaban con la luz del sol. Quise recostarme un rato al lado de la piscina, me gustaba tomar una siesta mañanera. Los rayos solares acariciaban mi pelo corto, sentía el aire abrazarme cálidamente y ahí me quedé, apaciblemente quieto, adormilado sobre la cama de hierba.

De pronto escuché un ruido al lado del garaje, mis instintos me impulsaron a averiguar qué estaba pasando. Con desconfianza caminé un poco hacia la calle, en dirección a la cerca del vecino. Recién nos habíamos mudado a esa casa y no sabíamos mucho sobre la seguridad del vecindario. Aproveché que la mitad de la cerca de madera estaba tumbada en el piso de hierba y la salté. La puerta del garaje del vecino estaba abierta, se me hizo fácil entrar a saludar, siempre me gustó la gente, yo me conocía de carácter dócil, alegre y sociable. El señor, ya muy adulto, se sorprendió al verme y yo intuí una sensación de miedo en su reacción que no me gustó. No sentí confianza en su mirada. Se acercó no sé para qué, yo di tres pasos atrás, el señor no se detuvo, siguió caminando hacia mí y estiraba su brazo como quien quiere tocarle la cabeza a un bicho raro: de pronto sentí miedo. De reojo –solo un poquito– giré la cabeza para medir la distancia de regreso, no era mucha. Cuando vi la mano del vecino encima de mis ojos, mi corazón dio un salto de angustia, ¡y ya no me contuve! De mi garganta salió un rugido grueso y profundo.

Mi boca se abrió intimidante. Las comisuras se hicieron visibles y dibujaron dos grandes curvas en la expresión de mi cara y la dentadura, ampliamente, mostró su mejor posición de amenaza: dientes, colmillos y molares aparecieron en función de defensa. Me abalancé rápidamente sobre el cuerpo del vecino. Él, visiblemente asustado, retrocedió y comenzó a gritar cosas que no eran palabras, eran discordancias verbales incomprensibles. Mi estrés aumentaba desenfrenadamente porque no me gusta sentirme tan vulnerable.

Cuando mi papá llegó corriendo, finalmente solté el pantalón del señor, que, incrustado en mis colmillos, me obligaba a girar la cabeza de un lado a otro sin permitirme recuperar mi libertad. Por un lado, el baileteo del cuerpo del vecino; por el otro, las palmadas de mi papá en mi cuerpo. Y yo, con todas mis fuerzas, retrocedía hacia la salida. Mi corazón palpitaba a mil revoluciones por segundo, mientras los tres intentábamos salir del aprieto en el que las circunstancias nos habían puesto.

El vecino llamó al 911 y llegaron los bomberos, la ambulancia y tres carros de policías. Todos, más algunos chismosos de la cuadra, tuvimos que esperar a que llegara la Animal Human Society. Traerían una orden de detención para animales peligrosos que atentaban contra la seguridad del vecindario. Cuando llegaron, la orden sentenciaba que yo debía de ser transferido de forma inmediata a la End of life Services. En otras palabras, iban a quitarme la vida debido a que yo era un perro de raza con alto riesgo para la comunidad. Mi familia no tuvo oportunidad de defender mi acto.

Nosotros, los caninos, no tenemos voz para explicar, para argumentar o para defender un hecho, y como mi familia no estaba cerca de mí cuando me salté la puerta de madera, no se les permitió interceder o proteger la vida de su mascota.

Desde la ventana de la patrulla que me transportaba, vi como mi hermanito, mi mamá y algunos vecinos, lloraban sin consuelo. Eso sí, los vecinos reunieron una suma considerable de dinero para una cremación privada, era el pago de mi eutanasia. Según ellos, porque el dolor era menor si sucedía lo más rápido posible. Y recordaron en su nota a mis papás que, en Tamarón, los ciudadanos aman a sus mascotas.

El monstruo dormido

El gran monstruo dormía, altivo, a las afueras del pueblo. Vestía el horizonte con su blancura y grandeza. Más o menos a cuarenta y ocho kilómetros de distancia, silencioso y altanero, esperaba que nos descuidáramos lo suficiente. Nosotros, adormilados por la vasta tormenta y el vaivén de las plantaciones de arroz y algodón, no dimos importancia al tremendo peligro que se nos venía encima.

Estuvo dormido por sesenta y nueve años, invadido por sueños exacerbados de furia y dolor; sueños contenidos, de libertad. Nadie supo interpretar su urgencia, su voz, su inminente cercanía.

Fue un miércoles. La tranquilidad de la noche era amenazante. Pasadas las nueve, la tienda de la esquina aún vendía chocolate y bizcochos de achira. Mi hija y yo caminábamos de regreso con una parva de cosas para desayunar la mañana siguiente, pues temprano saldríamos para la escuela.

—Ve preparándote para la cama Omaira, que se hace tarde, hija —dije inquieta, sin saber por qué. Mi abuela lo llamaba tener una "corazonada".

La niña buscó su piyama de Winnie the pooh insistentemente, abrió todos los cajones del ropero, la mesita de noche, y hasta debajo de la cama escarbó. No la encontró. Me miró con ojos de ternura suplicando por ayuda. Le pasé con la mano su piyama y el perrito de peluche con el que dormía.

Dos horas más tarde, inquieta en mi descanso, dormía bajo una luna en cuarto menguante, silenciosa y lánguida. En el sueño me veía corriendo y subía una lúgubre montaña rocosa. Me perseguían sombras irreconocibles: ¿árboles, animales, personas? No sabría decir. Mi corazón palpitaba ansioso, mi piel sudaba. Un escalofrío de terror recorrió mi cuerpo cuando escuché gritos de llanto a mis espaldas. Tuve miedo. No estaba segura de nada. Oía gritos de personas o mugidos de ganado, era el ruido de un profundo dolor y de una fúnebre agonía.

El monstruo vomitaba su furia. Soplando a mis espaldas, casi me alcanzaba; yo corría aún más rápido, la noche estaba oscura y fría. No me detuve a pensar, no intenté ayudar a los animales, ni pensé en regresar a casa para ayudar a mi hija... Ya no podía: ya era parte del lodo. Como ríos de agua espesa, corríamos a una velocidad vertiginosa, arrastrando rocas y fuego, levantando camiones enteros y llevándonos los techos de asfalto de los hogares de mi pueblo.

El cielo desapareció en el crepúsculo, ya no había nubes, ya no había horizonte, ya no había aire. Cerré los ojos y encogí mi cuerpo como cuando los gusanos de tierra se ven acorralados por manos depredadoras. Sentí mi ser arder y flotar en el aire, en la tierra, en el lodo... No sabría decir en qué momento supe que ya no estaba soñando.

Entre el lodo y la ceniza, el instinto de supervivencia me empujaba a velar por mi propia vida. A la velocidad de la avalancha, la mente simplemente silenció los pensamientos, las emociones y apegos. En la existencia desnuda, sin hija, sin esposo, sin hogar, buscaba la manera de sobrevivir. Me aferré al tronco de un árbol, esperé el alba de un nuevo día, sin saber con certeza si este iba a llegar.

Rescatistas, helicópteros y reporteros aterrizaron con los rayos del sol. Mi pueblo había sido sepultado vivo por el monstruo. Él, que un día le dio belleza, abundancia y vida, ese miércoles, con toda su fuerza y poder, nos borró de la faz de la tierra, como se borra una palabra mal escrita de una hoja de papel.

Poseída

Aún no me daba cuenta de su presencia, disfrutaba mi ocio y pasaba mucho tiempo rondando el jardín trasero. Ocupaba mi vaga somnolencia en hablar con las plantas, inquiriendo su percepción, su vitalidad y su nobleza; se dice de ellas que son el vacío fértil de lo esencial.

La suave compañía de mis únicas amigas, las plantas, daba sentido a mi rutina. Entonces un día entró un intruso a mi inercia: lo vi por primera vez esa mañana, era domingo, un día muy soleado. Yo iba con prisa a regar las plantas. Paré de golpe y curiosa, sentí que me sonreía, su mirada era profunda y fija, estática. Me veía con sus grandes ojos penetrantes y rugosos. Le devolví la mirada con curiosidad, pero de inmediato disimulé y pretendí que regaba mis plantas para no llamar su atención. No quería asustarlo, me gustó sentirme observada por él. Su enigmática presencia de pronto ocupó mis pensamientos, mi pulso aumentó. Quise hablarle, decirle que no corría peligro, que todo estaba bien, pero no lo hice. Pensé que mejor sería así, no intimidar mucho, no permitir el contacto... la naturaleza de las relaciones es un misterio que puede resultar peligroso.

Me levanté esa mañana esperando su visita. Miré a través de la ventana que da al canal, podía oír sus pisadas lentas, llenas de historia, llenas de hambre y sobrevivencia. El miedo es la emoción más primitiva que el ser humano conoce. Eso dicen. En mi caso no aplicaba porque me identificaba con su personalidad, su lucha por un hábitat propio y la terrible pesadez de su cuerpo. Al mirarlo desde la distancia hallaba un extraño placer al observar con detenimiento sus rasgos tan particulares, tan desconocidos.

Salí rápidamente al patio. Él caminó con lentitud, detuvo sus ojos en mí y me reparó, su enorme quijada se extendió mágicamente frente a mi absorta vista. No retrocedí. Con toda la paciencia se postró muy cerca del sofá que da a la entrada al patio. Nunca se había atrevido a llegar tan cerca, pensé, y me gustó, aún más, la audacia que describe a los reptiles.

Así quedó: en total quietud por un largo rato. Aproveché y decidí moverme un poco más cerca, vi algo que traía colgando en la comisura del hocico, era un trozo de carne vieja. No sé por qué, pero pensé de inmediato en el tejido cerebral que los vincula con la inteligencia, la memoria y la conciencia. No hizo ruido, cada vez más cerca y estático me reconocía.

Cautivada por su enigmática sagacidad y naturaleza, su brutal tamaño y sabiduría, prestaba toda mi atención a sus visitas. Lo sabía de carácter violento y depredador, y eran precisamente esos rasgos los que me acercaban a él. Encontraba una retorcida satisfacción al sentirme dominada por esa mirada binocular y penetrante. Pensé en cómo la soledad devora la profundidad de las almas ermitañas y fija melancólicamente un discurso interno, congruente, que justifica ese diálogo entre fuerzas imponentes. Me identifiqué con el pensamiento.

Me arrimé con pasos milimétricamente cercanos, deseando tocarlo para hacerle saber que estaba seguro. Él se movió sutilmente, lo suficiente para darme la tranquilidad que necesitaba para acercarme más hacia su cuerpo. Paré a una distancia pertinente, me pregunté cómo sería tener la dureza de su piel y poseer su naturaleza. Con la cercanía, mis palpitaciones aumentaron y las sentía en la garganta. Mi piel, cada vez más mojada por el sudor, tomó un color pálido verdoso. Justo ahí empezó mi mutación, aumentó mi presión sanguínea. Y mi lengua reseca me lamió los labios. Extendí entonces mi brazo y vi cómo los músculos contraídos casi lograban tocar su piel rígida y escamosa. Estábamos tan cerca el uno del otro que cualquier movimiento transfiguraría la unidad del ser, del todo. Y así fue.

La densidad de su aliento paralizó mis movimientos, era como si de pronto mi voluntad se hubiese esfumado, ya no había tregua, ni lucha, ya éramos uno. Ahora mi cuerpo clavado al suyo por fin sentía su rugosa y feroz piel, escuché un silbido agudo en mi cerebro que congeló mis pensamientos, oí sus pulmones respirar con victoria, sentí mi cuerpo bailar con movimientos transversales y en ese sentir, reposé.

Ahora mis ojos penetrantes y rugosos absorbían la sobrevivencia milenaria de los reptiles. Mi piel, con rígidas escamas, olía a azufre. Mi voz emitía un sonido imperceptible y vago que no me dejaba respirar. Me sentía poseída de manera etérea y simplemente convergí a su naturaleza.

En el patio trasero, frente al canal, en un mismo ser, nos arrastraríamos hacia el agua, en estado de reposo. Ahí engulliríamos inmóviles la comida y después la empujaríamos hacia el estómago. Encontraríamos así que los vínculos relacionales son un misterio que puede resultar fascinante.

"Quimeras"

Encuentro

La caída

Crista: vas caminando con paso acelerado, casi corriendo. Eres la clase de mujer que se permite estar tarde casi en todo; normalmente, algo se te cruza entre el tiempo y los quehaceres de la vida cotidiana. Llevas el cabello recogido en una cola de caballo bastante suelta, de las sienes se te paran mechones como hilos enredados que dejan entrever escamas blancuzcas en tu cuero cabelludo, así como áreas desnudas por la falta de pelo. Tu cuerpo se mueve sincrónicamente con la prisa, el brazo derecho esculca en tu bolsa a toda velocidad para sacar la servilleta donde habías apuntado la dirección, mientras tus ojos ven los pedazos de asfalto roto que hacen un hueco en el andén, obligándote a saltar casi encima del puesto de revistas ubicado a la derecha de la acera. Quieres esquivarlo, pero tus pobres reflejos te tiran al piso, y haces caer una buena cantidad de revistas.

Los ángeles

—Ring... Ring...

—¡Ay, ya voy! ¡Este timbre me pone los nervios de punta! Hola Crista, pasa y toma asiento. Una disculpa, algo pasa con ese timbre.

—Gracias, mmm, ¿aquí está bien?

—Está perfecto. Cuéntame sobre tus inquietudes.

—¿Así, en frío? A ver, me gustaría sentirme menos vacía, no disfruto nada ni de nadie, soy intolerante e irascible. A veces soy la persona que más odio en la faz de la tierra. ¡No comprendo por qué soy tan hostil con las personas más cercanas!

—Entiendo perfectamente. Mira querida, aquí en la doctrina de los ángeles vamos a dividir tu existencia en ciertas potestades, vas a encontrar respuestas a tus dudas, a tus miedos y a tu existencia. Aquí en tu plano finito de realidad vas a encontrarte a ti misma de forma suave, como las alas de los seres más privilegiados y gloriosos, tu espiritualidad va a hallar sus raíces y su fuente celestial.

—Um, ¿fuente celestial? Pero... yo no me siento merecedora de planos especiales. Tampoco los conozco, no sé. ¿Y si la influencia del ángel no me gusta?

—Tú no tienes que hacer nada, los ángeles te van a guiar. Ellos han estado desde el principio de la creación.

Crista, qué haces... recuerda que has leído sobre el ángel Sariel y te da como sustito. No, no empieces... entrégate: deja de jugar a la verdad y a la mentira. Escúchala, la idea es regular la frecuencia de las ondas del ruido mental. Ya lo habías decidido... Lo sabes Crista y aun así desconfías, te preguntas: ¿Y si finalmente no encuentro mi destino aquí tampoco?

—No, no, déjeme. Primero hablaré con mi coach y le aviso la próxima semana, ¿sí? En verdad no estoy segura de que sus ángeles me puedan ayudar.

—Está bien, tu divinidad te irá conduciendo. Tómate el tiempo que quieras, pero, a mí me gustaría que fueras primero con el chamán y participaras del ritual de curación en estado de trance. Definitivamente vas a conectarte contigo misma y con la madre de todas las madres. ¿Te gusta la idea?

—¡Sí, claro, me gusta! La llamo en la semana y le dejo saber cómo me siento.

El chamán

—Permiso, puedo pasar...

—¡No! ¡Atrás! ¡No tome asiento aún, quédese ahí parada para pasarle el sonajero herbal!

Ay dios, Crista, dónde te estás metiendo... ¿el sonajero herbal? Mira no más a este hombre, parece un loco. Eso te pasa por andar haciéndole caso a todo el mundo, Crista, Crista...

—Quieta. Él entrará en su cuerpo y le hará frente al espíritu que la trae en conflicto, así las vibras del universo la conectarán con su propio espíritu.

—Pero yo...

—¡Silencio! Usted está en un plano vacío e inerte, siento una energía pesada. Tome, mastique esto mientras entra en la misma vibración que su espíritu.

—¡Ay! Pero... ¿Cómo? ¿Me podría usted explicar primero cómo funciona esto? ¿Y por qué tengo que masticar estas hojitas? ¿Qué son?

—Chiss, Chiss...Veo que trae un espíritu muy castigador y tóxico. Acepte las posibilidades y suelte su ser a los dioses de la naturaleza. Especialmente al espíritu de la Madre Ayahuasca, para que la cure con su sabiduría y le muestre lo que usted tiene que ver, no se inquiete por nada, yo la conduzco. La cosmovisión amazónica tiene su propia alma y suelta el humo de la tierra y los espíritus, deje que su ser interior vuele.

—¿Co... cómo? ¡Oiga! ¿Pero qué me está echando encima? ¿No tiene que preguntarme primero? Solo quería que usted me ayudara con mi problema.

Agarra el suéter, Crista, y corre antes de que este...

—¡Yo ya me voy!

—No se vaya Crista, el resultado de su sensibilidad se va a potencializar y usted va a incursionar en un viaje de la mano de la madre selva. Al regresar de su viaje interior, todo va a tener más sentido. Yo la noto muy confundida, si usted cree que esto no es lo que busca, usted tiene la libertad de dejarlo. Pero su espíritu está inquieto y creo que usted ha de encontrarlo en algún lado. ¡No huya! Mire, tome esta tarjeta, busque a esta persona cuando esté lista para su crecimiento, buena suerte.

—Perdón, gracias de todas formas.

¿Por qué le pides perdón? ¡Y por qué le agradeces! Ah, claro, Crista, gracias por el susto y perdón por zoqueta.

Las luminarias

—Hola Crista. Toma asiento, ¿quieres un café?

—No, no, gracias, no tomo café.

—Cuéntame, ¿qué astros te traen por aquí?

—No sé mucho sobre astros y signos zodiacales, pero quiero saber si usted me puede ayudar.

Dile que estás confundida, Crista, e intranquila con tu conducta. Cuéntale que hieres a tus seres queridos, y cada vez estás más sola... Dile que las personas ya no te aguantan, que perdiste tu trabajo, que peleas mucho y que estás tan enojada que a todo el mundo le andas respondiendo con cuatro piedras en las manos. O mejor no le digas, deja que hablen los astros.

—Veamos qué alineación tienen los astros con tu destino, Crista. Te puedo dar una predicción astrológica precisa para que sepas cómo ven tu situación los astros y qué te depara el futuro de acuerdo con la rotación de los planetas en el momento exacto de tu hermoso nacimiento. ¿Sí sabes que hay cuatro tipos de elementos? Fuego, tierra, aire y agua. A algunos planetas se les llama generacionales, es porque pasan años en el mismo signo. Puede ser que Neptuno se haya quedado mucho tiempo en el tuyo... Ah, ya veo, tú eres aire, pero deseas lo fijo, lo estable, lo quieto, lo seguro.

¡Uf, qué calor hace aquí!

—Entiendo que usted quiere contarme sobre lo que conoce; eso sí lo entiendo y le agradezco, pero no es lo que yo busco, no, para nada. Tenga, aquí está el dinero de la sesión, muchas gracias.

Lo de los astros, lo de los signos y lo de los elementos, en serio, Crista, pero ¿qué tienen que ver con tu testarudez y arrogancia? Realmente estás bien frustrada, debes ver a alguien primero, alguien a quien no le has pedido una cita aún.

El encuentro

—Me ha costado mucho abrirte la puerta. Sé que no has sido mi primera opción y que no he venido a visitarte a tiempo; sé también que he evadido verte cara a cara. Creo que el miedo y la vergüenza de conocerte han dilatado nuestro encuentro.

—No está tan mal que sea hoy, te estaba dando tiempo para que te dieras cuenta de que al final del día, esta visita era inevitable. Tómala como el comienzo de una nueva forma de ver la vida y sus circunstancias. Lo que has pensado hasta ahora de ti es una forma de defender tu opinión sobre lo que quieres ser, no representa, realmente, lo que eres. Cada conflicto al que accedes, es una cara de tu propia naturaleza, te refugias en el argumento para justificarte, porque estás enojada con tu propia esencia, con la expectativa que tenías sobre ti. Eres una buscadora, te buscas para encontrar no el tener, ni el saber, sino para hallar el ser, la premisa del ser infinito dentro de ti.

—Sí, sí... estoy cansada de sentirme tan pesada, mi enojo me ha llevado a ser cruel y neurótica. De chica tuve que callar tanto y silenciar mi voz interior tanto, que ahora de adulta quiero gritarlo todo y a todos. El deber fue la prioridad fundamental en mi infancia, mientras que el espíritu del placer fue castrado y atropelló mi instinto natural de complacerme y de disfrutar. Esto me da tristeza y no sé qué hacer con este sentir.

—Reconcíliate con la persona que eres; para poder sanar debes comprender la enfermedad. El autoconocimiento te va a llevar a amarte y aliviarte, sin prejuicios, sin preceptos, sin apegos. Dedícate al conocimiento del "Yo soy" que te dará un valor de renuncia, de distancia, de introspección hacia la experiencia del aquí y ahora. Sal allá afuera y respira con amor y aceptación, no hay nada que puedas hacer para que el mundo sea como tú quieres que sea; sin embargo, hay mucho que puedes hacer para que tú seas la mejor versión para ese mundo en el que sueñas vivir, tu serás tu propio mundo. Hay mucho que puedes hacer para reconstruir esa persona que quieres. Pausa tu pensamiento y abre tu intuición, permítete sentir la nada, oler el viento y descansar. Deja de pensar.

—Crista, estás cansada, pero ya no hay prisa, ni hay lucha contra el tiempo. Reconoce tu espacio y déjate caer sobre el sofá de tela. Deja esa puerta abierta; esta es la última visita, la más importante. Cierra los ojos y descansa.

Ilusiones

Sentada en un sofá de su habitación, Elena escuchaba una canción que le recordó lo que no hacía mucho tiempo había cerrado: un pasado de maltrato, de humillaciones, de drogas y abandono emocional, donde ella no era más que una aventura insignificante y sin propósito. Una experiencia que, aunque lejana, reposaba en su mente como la historia de una pesadilla, un lienzo del pasado, finito, terminado. Apagó la radio, anuló los recuerdos y se levantó de la silla.

Por un segundo plasmó su pensamiento en el estrecho y nocivo vínculo que un día tuvo con Ariel. Pero sintió que ya era hora de mostrarse a sí misma que ese capítulo era cosa del pasado. Miró su reloj barato, el objeto marcaba las nueve menos diez minutos. La noche es joven, pensó, y rápidamente buscó algo sensual que vestir y algo de maquillaje que la iniciara en la aventura.

Revisó rápidamente su cartera, contabilizó uno a uno los objetos que necesitaba: dinero, labial, llaves, mentas, condón, identificación... Bajó su ceñido pantalón a la altura de las caderas y alborotó su cabello para ganarle volumen y seducción.

Mientras conducía hacia la disco, disfrutaba con una sonrisa la libertad que se regalaba esa noche. En sus venas, la sangre corría con velocidad y arrebato mientras ella, en su mente, imaginaba, de principio a fin, el desenlace de un encuentro nocturno de pasión y locura con algún desconocido.

En la oscuridad de la discoteca, la música rebasaba los decibeles aptos para comunicarse. Cientos de figuras, bailando estrechamente con movimientos curvos, lentos y seductores, acercaban cada piel, cada olor, cada sonrisa. Vio venir una figura masculina que se acercaba bailando seductoramente desde el centro de la pista de baile. Una ráfaga de palpitaciones le avisó que era momento de estar atenta, de estar dispuesta; hacía muchos años no sentía algo parecido. Elena sentía la euforia de su piel acechando al hombre, no lo conocía: ello la hacía arder de placer. Mientras bailaba con movimientos lentos, lo miraba con la sed con que un adicto observa su droga. Se acercó a su alto y bien formado cuerpo. Bailaban tan cerca que podía oler su sudor, sentir su vibración, escuchar su seductor pensamiento... Él la tomó por los hombros y la volteó de espaldas, entrelazó sus manos y las reposó sobre sus pechos; sus pezones se tensaron mientras la movía al ritmo de la música electrónica. Ebria de erotismo, se entregaba a sus mandatos sensoriales, las manos entrelazadas bajaron... Respiró su vientre y un torrente de sangre le llegó al cerebro, ya no escuchaba la música, sólo sentía la sensación del placer en sus entrañas, en lo más profundo de su estómago. Escuchaba sus propios gemidos venir ahogados. Las manos del íntimo extraño bailaban con movimientos seductores sobre su abdomen. Desde atrás, ella sentía su pene robusto y erecto. Frágil, se desvanecía lentamente de placer y éxtasis. Él, sin anunciar y con audaz desempeño, allanaba con sus manos el pantalón de Elena, deslizándolas lentamente, la provocaba con su sexualidad feroz y simple. Ella, entonces, se encontró en un mar cálido y espeso que, accediendo a los sentidos de la aventura, dilataba su sexo, su intimidad. La boca de Elena se entreabrió con un gemido mientras los dedos de él danzaban lujuriosos y juguetones en su pelvis. Sus cuerpos adheridos por la música y por el placer de la noche, se perdían ferozmente en un mar incontrolable de sensaciones. No había testigos, no había objetos, no había etiquetas, no había planes para un futuro. Estaban en una dimensión donde solo ellos dos podían existir en una constante universal. El mundo se apagó, los absorbió un gran hueco negro que giraba en un hiperespacio donde cada vez se escuchaban menos la música, las voces y la presencia de un lugar.

Al día siguiente, Elena despertó triunfante en su cama. Un rayo de luz entraba por la ventana entreabierta. Se sentó con la espalda erguida y estiró los brazos hacia el infinito, después los abrió a sus anchas y ahí los dejó, como expandiendo su pecho para meterle todo el oxígeno del universo en una sola inhalada.

Pensó en llamar a su hermana y contarle, se detuvo un instante y la imaginó preguntando: ¿Pero lo conoces? ¿Es de buena familia? ¿Trabaja? ¿Quedaron en algo? O vas a seguir en lo mismo...

Convencida de que todo tiempo presente es mejor, cerró los ojos y sonrió con gratitud, despojada de toda expectativa, satisfecha.

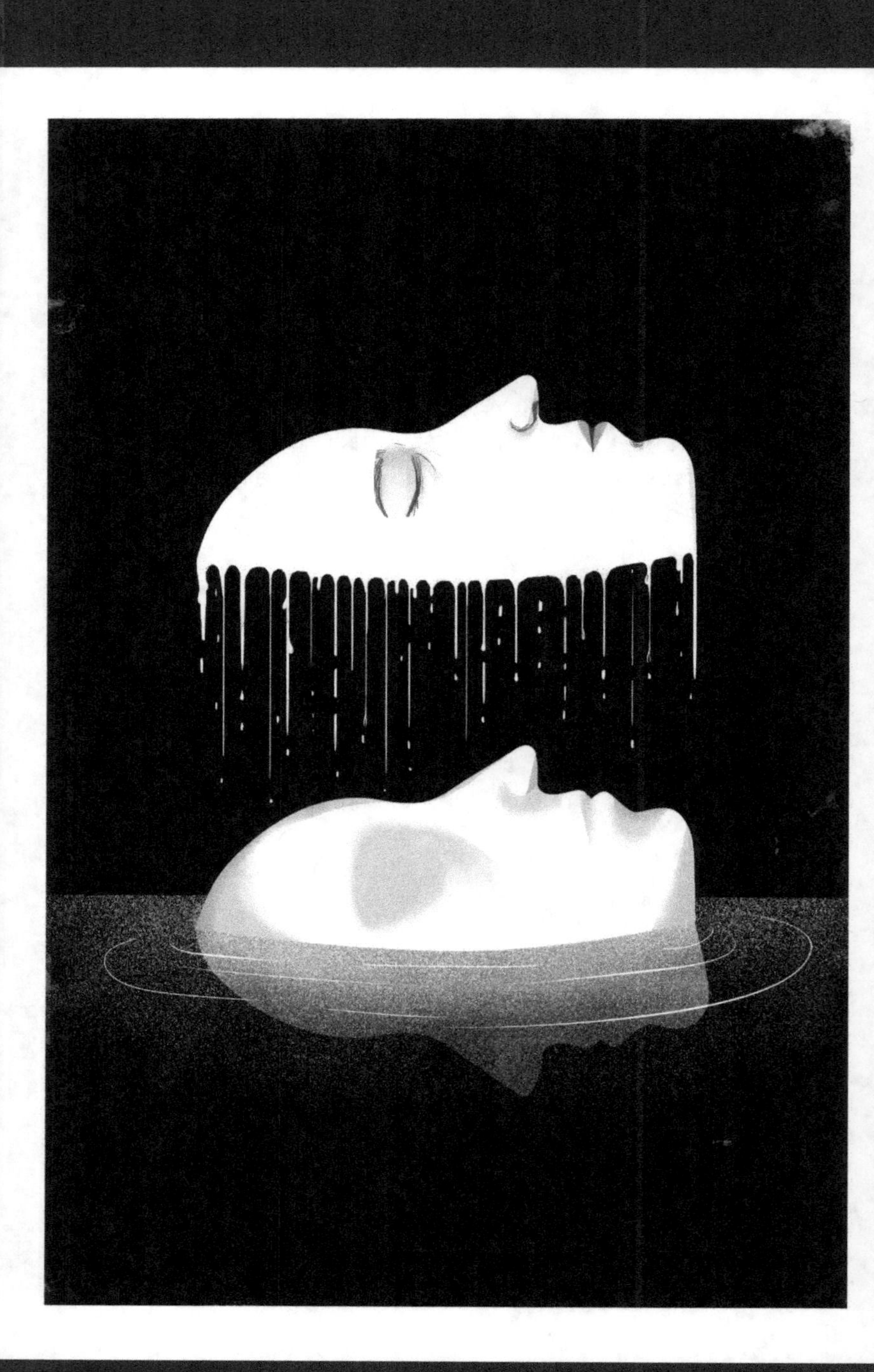

Identidad perdida

Mi vida es un puro errar

Alejandra Pizarnik

Despierto de un sueño profundo para encontrar que no estoy en la cama del hospital al que llegué herida e inconsciente. Empiezo a recordar...

El lugar es angosto, acolchonado con una tela suave como el satín. Está totalmente oscuro, sin ventilación. Mi cuerpo inmóvil y frío finalmente encuentra la soledad, no me asusta. Pienso que Irene, al fin, ha escuchado mis súplicas, ya no tendré que soportar esta vida a la que yo misma me he arrastrado.

Se acercan muchas voces, indistinguibles, escucho una en particular que empieza a llorar: es mi mamá. Lamenta mi ausencia, me pide perdón por sus negligencias en mi crianza. Con ella recuerdo mi infancia, mi adolescencia, las veces que me escapé de la escuela, las veces que le robé dinero para invitar a alguna amiga una cerveza. Recuerdo las noches que no volví a casa a dormir, y la dejé plena de preocupación y angustia. Sus cortos pasos se escuchan lejos.

Una voz masculina me saca de los remordimientos. Es Jorge, mi primer novio, él no llora, sólo habla con tono pausado, casi susurra.

—Lila, mi amor, no puedo creer que ya no estés con nosotros, ¿qué pasó? Te dije que siempre estaría para ti, que siempre iba a estar esperando tu llamada... lamento no haberte besado con ternura una última vez... sabes que fuiste mi único amor.

Al escucharlo, mi corazón tiembla. Siempre quise buscarlo y pedirle perdón por haberme acostado con su mejor amigo: sé que eso lo desgarró. Éramos muy chicos, nunca he sentido más vergüenza que aquel día en el que Jorge abrió la puerta del baño en casa de sus padres y nos pilló. Me sentí muy mal cuando, a raíz del enojo, se salió de la escuela y no quiso más ser parte del grupo: ¡De nosotros, que éramos sus únicos amigos! Escuchar sus palabras me llena de tranquilidad y de paz. Perdida en mis pensamientos, no me percato de que se ha ido, pero ya es otra voz la que me habla, muy cerca de la pared de mi encierro.

—Mija, usted siempre con las bobadas de no contar sus cosas, siempre tan callada, sufriendo sola, ¿qué pasó, mi nena? Me hubiera llamado, hubiera venido a verme, usted sabía que yo nunca la iba a juzgar por nada. Me duele mucho su partida, de pronto siento que debí buscarla más, hacer presencia en su dolor... ahora entiendo que no era arrogancia suya, simplemente usted no sabía cómo pedir ayuda. La quiero mucho, mija, que Dios la guarde en su amor y la perdone grandemente.

Es mi tía Carol, creí que me odiaba con su alma llena de vicios religiosos. Escucho pasos, muchos más pasos, se alejan y se acercan. No sé que está pasando allá afuera. Siento frío y la cabeza me da vueltas. Sin embargo, yo estoy tranquila, mis palpitaciones son pausadas y rítmicas. Escuchar la voz de las personas cercanas y saber qué pensaban sobre mí es realmente reparador. Pasan varias amigas, algunas cercanas que casi no frecuento, otras distantes con las que hablo de vez en cuando. Escucho vecinos y antiguos maestros. ¿Cómo puede ser que tanta gente se haya tomado el tiempo para venir a despedirme?

—No sé qué decirte flaca, de pronto sería bueno comenzar por pedirte perdón... pero tengo la seguridad de que, desde el cielo o el infierno, donde sea que estés: ¡vas a refutar y contradecir todo lo que yo te diga! Espero que no hayas sufrido en el momento de tu muerte, yo sé que no terminamos bien, pero esta última vez tú me provocaste. ¿Cómo es posible que hayas llegado así de ebria? Ni siquiera te podías parar por ti misma. Y ese hombre que te trajo ¡ni lo conocías! Fueron muchas veces, flaca, muchas cosas. Lamento haberte golpeado mientras estabas inconsciente... siento mucho las veces que te pegué, las que te grité, las que te ridiculicé. Lamento no haberte valorado. Cuando te llevé al hospital no pude decir que era tu marido, me hubieran llevado preso, flaca, por eso te dejé tirada. ¡Te pido perdón! Nunca imaginé que fueras capaz de hacerte daño. Te buscamos por todas partes, en el hospital no se dieron cuenta de que te fuiste, tu familia estaba desesperada, flaca. Siempre fuiste tan voluntariosa y rebelde, mira... de no haber sido por Irene que nos avisó, flaca...

No puedo creer lo que oigo. Es él. Estoy paralizada. Ha decidido entrar a "despedirse". Lo conozco tan bien que siempre supe que buscaría la forma de llegar, en medio de tantas personas que lo odian, que estuvieron tan en contra de esta relación, que siempre le apostaron a un final nefasto y por poco aciertan porque casi me mata a golpes.

Mis palpitaciones aumentan súbitamente, siento un sudor frío que empapa mi espalda, mis lágrimas corren hacia las sienes. Esta visita, este último adiós me hace hervir la sangre. De pronto este angosto lugar vestido de satín, que ahora es mi refugio, me incomoda, me amenaza. Me advierte con soberbia sobre la posibilidad de develar la realidad. Tengo dificultad para respirar, empuño mis manos para paralizar mi ímpetu, mi pecho se hace pequeño por la necesidad de aire, quiero vomitar. El espacio se reduce aún más y me siento extraña a mí misma, siento que floto atrapada en mi propio cuerpo, en mi propio engaño.

Golpean la madera, reconozco la voz, es Irene. Está enojada.

—Ya vi al pendejo. ¡Descarado! ¿Cómo logró entrar? Todo va a estar bien, aguanta amiga, estoy aquí para ti, estamos juntas en esto... No dejes que se salga con la suya, aguanta.

Tengo que confiar en ella. Irene tiene razón, sabe que estoy desesperada.

De forma abrupta levantan mi escondite: ahora el ataúd se balancea de un lado a otro. La cabeza me da vueltas. Finalmente, me ubican en una superficie plana. No veo la hora de que la funeraria cierre. No veo la hora de que termine toda esta farsa. Irene me calma, me habla en clave, me dice que en pocos minutos se abrirá mi cielo y veré el fruto de la salvación.

No estoy segura. Como siempre, demasiado tarde me doy cuenta de que yo misma me he metido en este embudo. Ahora que escucho lo que todos piensan de mí, ahora que veo que están arrepentidos, que me valoran, ahora que me siento apreciada... Ahora, sin mi vida, me doy cuenta de que siempre tuve la oportunidad de vivir de la mejor forma, pero nunca quise tomar las riendas. Y ahora es demasiado tarde.

Una vez que todos crean que entré al crematorio, saldré por la puerta de atrás y seré nadie. De Lila ni siquiera habrán quedado las cenizas.

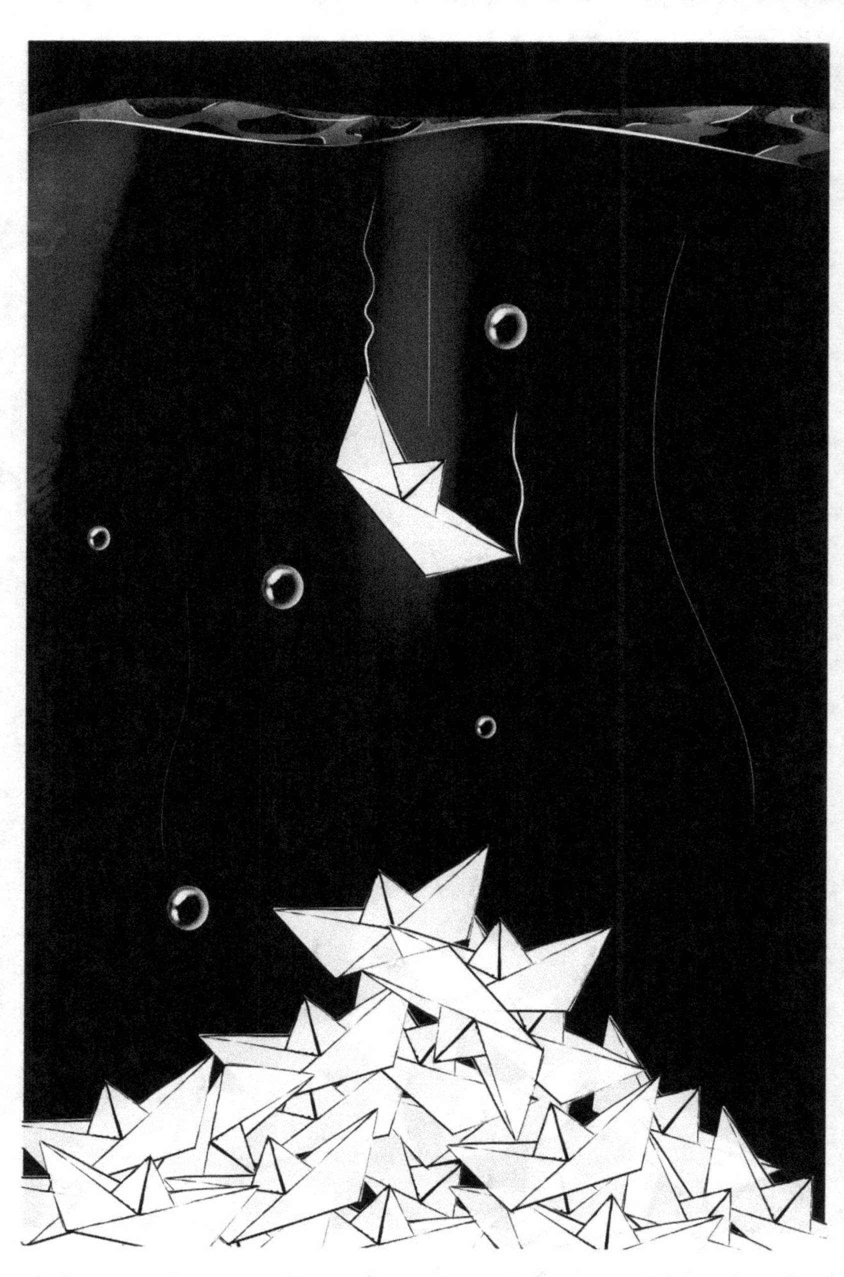

Barquitos de papel

Es al separarse cuando se siente y se comprende la fuerza con la que se ama.

Fiódor Dostoievski

El momento más emocionante era cuando ya todo estaba listo: los fiambres, la gaseosa, la leña para el fogón, platos y vasos plásticos, y una pelota vieja de futbol para jugar el pase. Corríamos y nos amontonábamos en la carrocería llenos de alegría por el día que nos esperaba. Para nosotros los paseos de olla eran "el gran viaje", una vez por mes, los domingos. Para ella, eran el gran regalo de amor hacia sus hijos; la aventura y la alegría en el río.

Montábamos todo en un camión de estacas que mi madre rentaba para que nos llevara en la mañana y nos recogiera en la tarde, ella aprovechaba para lavar la ropa sucia del mes. Mientras lavaba en el río, los hijos organizábamos lo demás: la hoguera, los tendederos, las mantas para sentarnos a comer; y así cada grupo tenía algo que hacer. Primero construíamos un charquito con piedras para los más chicos, ahí jugaban hasta quedar como uvas pasas. Los grandes nos encargábamos de la comida mientras nos entreteníamos contando chistes y haciendo payasadas para divertir a mi mamá que hacía brazo azotando las cobijas sobre la piedra para que —según ella— quedaran más limpias. De vez en cuando le echábamos ojo a los más chicos para asegurarnos de que estaban bien y de que no se salieran del charquito. Así fue hasta que un domingo, el río Pance nos hizo una mala jugada.

Esto fue lo que pasó. Mis hermanos menores y yo jugábamos en la piscina del río. Fermín, como era el mayor, nos había dicho que si queríamos algo le gritáramos y que por nada del mundo nos saliéramos de las piedras, pero, cuando el barquito se fue por entre un rotico, yo miré a Alba y ella me decía algo, pero no podía escucharla porque el río hacía mucha bulla. En eso me jaló del pelo hacia ella y eso me dolió mucho, también me dio rabia; le quité su mano de mi cabeza y le dije que me dejara en paz, que quería alcanzar mi barquito. A ella no le importó, solo decía que le hiciera caso, que era peligroso. Miré hacia donde estaba mi mamá lavando, pero ella ni siquiera podía vernos. Mis hermanos grandes tenían la música muy alto y se reían a carcajadas, así que yo traté de alcanzar mi barquito sosteniéndome de una de las piedras.

Alba, de apenas diez años, trató de ayudarme tirando de mi camiseta por la espalda. Yo estiré mi brazo, pero la piedra se movió y me hizo perder el equilibrio; mi flacuchento cuerpo se deslizó entre las piedras y ante el jaloneo de la corriente del río. Alba no pudo sujetarme más. Sentí una corriente de agua entrar por mi boca, mi corazón comenzó a latir más rápido y fuerte; de pronto algo me golpeó la espalda, mi mamá pasó por mi pensamiento. Sabía que la corriente me estaba llevando, yo quería prenderme de las ramas de los árboles que colgaban en la orilla, pero mis manos se deslizaban por el barro pantanoso. Cuando trataba de sacar la cabeza del agua, mi cuerpo se deslizaba entre una y otra piedra y ya no podía controlarlo. Levanté mi brazo así, como mi mamá nos había enseñado, pero la corriente era tan fuerte que mi cabeza se pegaba contra las piedras. En un breve instante, a lo lejos pude ver mi barquito. Quise llorar, pero como mis ojos estaban dentro del agua no sentí las lágrimas. Seguí tragando hasta que quise vomitar y ya no sentí más la lucha, mi cuerpo estaba muy pesado: me rendí.

Cuando mi hermanito murió, ninguno de nosotros imaginó que en la soledad de su ausencia también perderíamos a nuestra madre. Ella, que siempre fue el espíritu de las reuniones, también se había ido. Fue un domingo de junio el último paseo que tuvimos, de eso hace ya cinco años, y no pasa un día sin que la culpa nos recuerde el ímpetu del agua y lo irremediable de un descuido.

Nuestra madre trabajaba, iba y venía, llegaba a casa y cocinaba, salía a la tienda, compraba mercado, regresaba a la casa, sacudía el balcón, regaba las plantas, lavaba la fachada, volvía a entrar, revisaba alguna esquina, tendía las camas, limpiaba un jarrón o lloraba una balada. Tarde en la noche la escuchábamos susurrar una canción: "Los niños no se mueren, se nos van al cielo, quedan en el alma y se ponen alas, y vuelan muy cerca. Los niños no mueren, se van por un tiempo a juntar estrellas y nacen de nuevo en otro pequeño". Yo sufría al ver su dolor, quería leer su alma, poder curarla y consolarla como el Stárets Zosima hizo con la mujer que perdió a su hijito.

Mi madre salió una mañana a visitar a una vecina que estaba enferma en el hospital. Cuando regresó traía en sus brazos un bulto de ropa, nos dijo que era de su amiga. Fue extraño, pues desde la muerte de Néstor, ella no había vuelto a lavar, siempre nos pedía a alguno de nosotros que nos encargáramos de su ropa. Celebramos mucho que en un acto de solidaridad volviera a ser ella y volviera a realizar actividades como esta, sin emociones dañinas. Pero al día siguiente ya no fue a trabajar, ni siquiera abrió la puerta de su cuarto. Desde adentro y con una voz de susurro contestó que estaba bien, que siguiéramos haciendo la cena sin ella, que más tarde ella nos alcanzaría. La escuchábamos cantar: "Los niños no mueren, se van por un tiempo a juntar estrellas y nacen de nuevo en otro pequeño". No nos acompañó a cenar.

En la madrugada la escuché susurrar: chsss, chsss; pero no dije nada. Eran las seis y media de la mañana cuando un llanto escandaloso nos despertó de golpe, salimos asustados hacia el cuarto de mi mamá, la puerta estaba con llave o atrancada:

—¡Mamá, por favor, abra la puerta!

—¿Qué pasó? ¡Estamos bien, vuelvan a dormir! —contestó con voz nerviosa.

—¡Mamá, por favor! ¿Por qué hay un bebé con usted?

—No hagan ruido, lo están asustando; déjennos tranquilos. En un ratito se calma su hermanito. Chsss, chsss, chsss.

El bebé siguió llorando, era un llanto agudo y estridente, como un grito. Estábamos realmente preocupados y sin saber qué hacer. Mil preguntas de dolor y miedo llegaban a nuestras mentes; ¿De quién era ese bebe? ¿Lo había sacado del hospital, era el bulto de ropa sucia? ¿Cómo lo estaba alimentando? ¿Qué esperaba qué hiciéramos?

Una hora después nuestra casa era el escenario del barrio; aglomerados en la entrada estaban la policía, el personal del hospital y los vecinos, que, morbosos, querían saber qué había hecho nuestra madre.

Cuando todo acabó, entramos a la habitación de mi madre y pudimos ver que tenía una colección de barquitos de varios tamaños, colores y modelos, algunos de ellos hechos con tronquitos de madera.

Fin